FATE OF THE BOLD

FATE OF THE BOLD

D. S. COOPER

Fate of the Bold
Copyright © 2018 by D. S. Cooper

All rights reserved. No part of this book may be used or reproduced in any manner whatsoever including Internet usage, without written permission of the author.

This is a work of fiction. The names, characters, places, or events used in this book are the product of the author's imagination or used fictitiously. Any resemblance to actual people, alive or deceased, events or locales is completely coincidental.

Copyedited by Jennifer Blackwell-Yale

Print and e-book formatting by Maureen Cutajar
www.gopublished.com

Cover design by Ebook Launch
www.ebooklaunch.com

For more information:
www.dscooperbooks.com

Print ISBN: 978-0-9984100-3-6
E-book ISBN: 978-0-9984100-2-9

For Jill Colletti
"Ruby"

*"If fate means for you to lose,
give him a good fight anyhow."*

Casuals of The Sea
WILLIAM MCFEE

Alicia ...

"I was never meant to know that my mother was the famous Cuban artist Pilar Vasquez. I was taken from her as an infant and raised with no knowledge of her or the country of my birth."

Why were you taken?

"To hide the terrible deeds of powerful men and weak courts."

Is Pilar still alive?

"With the help of a good man I will find her. Connor's flaws are many, but he is a good man."

What is a good man?

"A good man revels in his own flaws until his better nature is desperately needed by another."

PROLOGUE

Wednesday, June 22, 1953

El Vedado, Havana, Cuba

The moon had climbed high into the heavens before Pilar heard the heavy gate between the courtyards open. A gentle breeze stirred the curtains in her window. Would Ernesto come to her this night?

She trembled at the thought of him breathing on her neck, touching her, being closer than ever, and she knew that on this night she would not pull away. She would not laugh and tease any longer. If Ernesto came to the balcony this night and invited her down to the courtyard, she would climb down and be with him.

Her excitement was unbearable when he whistled like a nightingale and called to her from the window.

"Pilar, I am here for you."

They climbed down together and he led her past the fountain to the flower garden where they once played hide-and-seek. There, behind the gold duranta and almond verbena, her beauty was revealed in the glow of the moon.

"Ernesto, you are a nasty boy," she said in the flower garden where they had played all their lives, apart from the world beyond the walls.

"How is this bad?"

"My father will kill you."

"*Que sera sera,*" he said.

"You would die to be with me?"

"Of course, I would a thousand times."

The distant music of a dozen casinos drifted across the night sky of Havana and down into the courtyard. They were fourteen years old, first cousins, and their parents were at one of those parties.

"Gretel will find us," Pilar said.

"She is an old woman sleeping," Ernesto said. "She will never find us here."

"Yet I feel that she is always watching, even now."

"Aunt Gretel is a mean old woman, never married. There is no joy there."

"She will tell our parents."

"No one will ever know. No one knows where we are. Just us."

"I want to tell the world."

They had never breathed so deeply.

That was when the form of a woman in a long black dress trampled the beautiful duranta to loom above them. The moon behind Gretel made her appear large and menacing.

"*Pecado mortal!*" she said when she reached down to grab Pilar by the arm. Gretel pulled her charge apart from Ernesto so forcefully that it would leave a bruise. *Mortal sin!*

"*Eres el diablo!*" Gretel said, raising the switch in her other hand to Ernesto. *You are the devil!*

Ernesto did not shirk from the switch. He stood up and faced Gretel, which inflamed her rage. He flinched when it stung his cheek and raised welts but he did not turn away. He forced his hands to remain down at his side in ultimate defiance while she beat him.

"*Tu propio primo!*" she said. "How could you be so evil?" *Your own cousin!*

With each sting of the switch Ernesto understood that Gretel had anticipated the moment for years, watching and waiting as he and Pilar played hide-and-seek in their family's adjoining courtyards—following at a distance as they held hands and strolled on the *Malecon* at sunset, pushing them together—knowing the outcome.

"*Chico horrible!*" Gretel said. *Horrible boy.*

Their parents might say, *remember, she is your cousin, almost a sister.* But not Gretel. She would watch in silence as the children approached maturity in two of the grandest mansions in Havana, delighting in the certainty that one day their play would become amorous and that she would be there to expose their sin.

"*Chico repugnante*! Your parents must send you far away to the Sierra Maestra! You are one for the mountains, *disgusting boy*!"

Fifty-two years later…

CHAPTER 1

Wednesday, March 16, 2005

An Ace in the Hole

No matter how many deaths we cause at the same instant as our own—in Connor's case it might be hundreds of innocent men, women, and children—we all meet our maker alone. Captain Connor Laird knew this well because like all airline pilots he had rehearsed escaping from death on a grand scale many times. So, when his Boeing 737 fell out of the clouds over Old San Juan with an intense conflagration consuming the tail section of the airplane, saving his own butt was no minor consideration.

Other than his ardent desire to stay alive, Connor was out of ideas. Nothing in the cockpit was working as it should. His movements of the controls had become meaningless gestures as the wings skirted over the old city, narrowly missing the massive stone ramparts and guard turrets of La Fortaleza at the entrance to the harbor. No matter what he tried, the Boeing kept speeding straight toward the Bacardi rum factory on the far side of the ship channel, and in the final moments the giant black bat on the roof of the famous distillery grew larger and larger ahead of them until it filled the jet's windshield.

When the nose of the Boeing rifled dead-center through the rum factory, the screens inside the cockpit went dark, the alarms went silent, and the massive hydraulic jacks ceased shaking and tilting *the box*—which was what pilots called the full-motion simulator at Flight Safety International in Orlando, Florida.

Then the lights came on and Alicia Vasquez was sitting in the copilot's seat next to Connor staring straight ahead, shocked. This routine simulator check-ride was meant to return them to flying status after an incident at San Juan four months earlier and was not supposed to end in disaster.

"What could we have done differently?" Ali said when she turned her green eyes toward her captain.

"Nothing," Connor said. "That was bullshit." Connor turned around and leveled both barrels at the instructor pilot sitting behind them. "What the hell was that? You're not supposed to give us a non-survivable situation."

"Sorry, Connor. If it makes you feel any better, that wasn't part of the check-ride."

"It wasn't? Because if that was your idea of a sick joke, I'm going to take you out behind the building and explain that I'm not amused."

"It wasn't me, Connor. Your chief pilot made me run you through that program."

The straight-talking chief pilot of Anthem Airways was waiting for Connor and Ali when they came down the stairs from the box.

"Cool your jets, Connor," Dan Ward said. "I had to see how you two would react."

"React to what? That was a load of crap, Dan. Nobody can survive when a bomb blows the tail off their airplane."

"Exactly," Dan said. "I had to see how you would react to a nightmare scenario. Jamming the controls and launching you into the Bacardi factory was a nice touch, don't you think?"

"I think you're a spring-loaded prick," Connor said, not appreciating the swipe at his alcoholic past.

"Why would you do that to us?" Ali said. She was about half Connor's age and her youthful charm was a sharp counter to his sometimes-flinty manner.

"Because Connor Laird is the luckiest pilot alive," Dan said. "Did you know that a SAM-21 missile went right past the canopy of his

Navy A-7 attack jet and knocked his wingman out of the sky over Hanoi?"

"I thought that was just a hangar-flying story," Ali said, looking at Connor.

"No, it actually happened that way," Connor said. "But my wingman must not be sore about it—because I married his sister while he was a POW."

"See what I mean?" Dan said. "You had an ace up your sleeve again. Then just recently you did something really stupid and tried to take off in a thunderstorm at San Juan but ended up going off the runway and planting the nosewheel of a perfectly good Boeing 737 in the mud."

"We would have stopped in plenty of time if the anti-skid brakes were working properly," Ali said.

"Right," Dan said. "Let's not forget who neglected to arm the anti-skid brakes that day, First Officer Vasquez. Wasn't that your responsibility per the checklist? Then two professional pilots ignored the caution light signaling that the brakes weren't armed when you advanced the thrust levers. Which is telling me that I had two very distracted humans in that cockpit that morning. So, what went on in that hotel room the night before?"

"Nothing," Connor and Ali said, in lock-step.

"Really, Connor? One of your cabin crew testified that he saw Ali coming out of your hotel room half-dressed that morning, hours before the incident."

"Screw Jason Piccard," Connor said. "Who cares what that fairy testifies?"

"Take it easy," Ali said. "Getting mad won't help, Connor."

"The lawyers who are suing us, that's who cares," Dan said. "You two can do whatever you want on your own time, but you can't jump between the sheets together on a trip. The company human relations policy is perfectly clear on that score."

"This job was a lot more fun in the good old days, wasn't it, Dan? Remember the fun times we had when we were both flying for Pan Am?"

"Yeah, I remember," Dan said. "But that's ancient history. The only thing that's going to save you this time is how the news media painted you like a big hero for saving the passengers."

"That was just dumb luck," Connor said. "How was I supposed to know there was a bomb in the galley that was going to blow the tail off the airplane as soon as we abandoned the flight?"

"I wish I knew the answer to that," Dan said. "Pretty much everyone in the airline industry is asking how you managed to pull that one off. Tell me the truth, old buddy, do you have ESP or something? A sixth sense to pull your butt out of the sling every time?"

"I cancelled the takeoff because we got hit by a microburst," Connor said. "I had no idea there was a bomb onboard."

"Okay," Dan said. "If you say so. But I don't want you two bidding for the same flights on the April schedule."

"What?" Ali said. "Why not?"

"You know that you're being sued by some of your passengers, don't you?"

"Of course, they're suing us," Connor said, "even though we saved their lives. It's the new American way."

"No good deed goes unpunished," Ali said.

"Listen to reason," Dan said. "For your own good you shouldn't fly together for a while."

"I don't think so," Connor said. "This is still a union shop so you can't tell two fully qualified pilots they can't fly together."

"I knew you'd say that," the chief pilot said with a shrug. "Here's my best comeback, Connor—I'm retiring in two months. Why don't you take my job? It's yours if you want it."

"No thanks, pal. I was never good at flying a desk—the landings are brutal."

Self-defense

Special Agent Rene Garcia was waiting for the pilots when they walked into a conference room at the FBI office in North Miami Beach that afternoon. As usual he was dressed more like a gangster than a cop—with a colorful short-sleeve shirt and gold chains—when he extended a muscular arm to shake their hands.

"This is your lucky day, Connor," Garcia said, pushing a handgun case and a gold badge across the table, along with a sheaf of paper. "We're returning your Glock and Federal Flight Deck Officer credentials so you can return to flying with a weapon in the cockpit. Sign here."

"Great," Connor said.

"So, it's official?" Ali said. "We're no longer suspects in the bombing?"

"That's right, you'll get letters at your home addresses," Garcia said. "Which reminds me, are you still using that post office box in Glen Burnie?"

"Yes," she said. "I'll buy a condo in Annapolis when things settle down. Until then there are a lot of Residence Inns in Maryland and Virginia."

"Good for you. But what's this about your adopted mother selling the house in Maryland and moving back to Estonia?"

"It was a total surprise to me," Ali said. "Rose left everything behind and hardly said good-bye."

"It was a surprise to me too," Garcia said. "So, tell me straight up, do you stand by your statement that Rose never knew you had been kidnapped as an infant?"

"Now, I really don't know," Ali said. "We'll have to talk about that someday."

"Don't go to Estonia for that conversation," Garcia said. "Remember that Nikoli Volkov is permanently banned from entering the United States but he can travel freely in Europe. To be blunt—you probably won't survive another encounter with the Russian state security services."

Ali only nodded in response and for a few seconds nothing was said.

"Let me ask you something," Connor said, breaking the silence. "Since we're in the clear for the bomb on our flight, who are the real suspects?"

"All indications are that Puerto Rican separatists—the *Fuerzas Armadas de Liberacion Nacional*—put that explosive device on your flight. The assumption is that they were after the statehood delegation onboard."

"Well, if you ask me," Connor said, "I don't believe the FALN acted alone. Where would a bunch of yahoos in Puerto Rico get Czechoslovakian explosives?"

"Why don't you leave the detective work to me," Garcia said. "I came down from my office in Rhode Island because I wanted to be the one to get your pistol out of the evidence room here and hand it back to you. I haven't given up on this case."

"Fine," Connor said. "I hope you're still looking at the Cubans and the Russians."

"The reality is politics, Connor. Since we never found that picture of Ernesto with the microdot that Volkov came to collect, some of our elected officials in Congress refuse to believe that the Russians were directly involved. So, I have to move very carefully and the best thing you can do is to lay low."

"You're asking a lot," Connor said. "I take it personally when someone attempts to kill me and my passengers."

"Me too," Ali said. "I hope you don't expect me to stop looking for Pilar and Ernesto. I hope to someday know what actually happened to my real parents."

"I get all that," Garcia said. "And I know that Lorraine is working on a book about this whole episode. All I ask is that you all keep a lid on this thing until we figure out who all the bad actors were."

"Fine," Connor said. "But I hope that someone above your pay grade gives a shit that the Russians wanted to cover up a thirty-year-old drug smuggling case so badly that they tried to kill seven Americans at Little Shady Key, including two kids and Ambassador-at-Large Bertram Calhoun. And by the way, if I ever see Nick Volkov again, I'm going to shoot him, no questions asked."

"Maybe you should give back that Glock, Connor. I don't want to arrest you for murder."

"It will be in self-defense," Connor said. "And trust me, if Volkov gets his sights on me first, it's lights out for me. I get that, for sure."

Newport, Rhode Island

Bennett Ransom Laird's problem was that none of the kids at Rogers High School would believe him. How could they, with his story of CIA drug smugglers, Cuban freedom fighters, and the Russian spy he had helped his father and his Uncle Ransom defeat in hand-to-hand combat? So he had never told the whole story of the home invasion on Little Shady Key. But when he surreptitiously entered the back door of the animal hospital where Natalie Lopes worked after school, he had the proof of his exploits—he hoped—tucked into the pages of his chemistry textbook.

Finders keepers, Bennett had thought when Nikoli Volkov dropped the snapshot of Ernesto with the microdot attached. In all the confusion no one saw him push it into his shorts. Now all he had to do was read the secret message and the mystery would be solved.

"You shouldn't be in here," Natalie said, when he appeared among the cages and shelves of animal food and supplies in the back room.

"You're not happy to see me?"

"I've got to feed the boarders. And you know Doc's rule, no boyfriends."

"Doc would never turn away a kid with a science question," Bennett said.

"That's true, but you need to come in the front door."

"I don't really have a question," he said, opening his chemistry textbook to show her the old black-and-white snapshot of a teenager standing in front of a biplane. "I need a microscope."

"Let me see that," Natalie said. "Is the dot still attached?"

"It's in the margin, with the date. See?"

"Are you sure this is Ali's father, Ernesto?"

"See what someone wrote on the back, *Ernesto, Santiago, October 1957*."

"Why are you carrying this around, Ben?"

"I wanted to read the dot with one of our microscopes at school, but they weren't powerful enough."

"Ernesto's kind of cute," Natalie said, handing the snapshot back. "But you should have given this to your grandfather right away. The ambassador will know what to do with it."

"Maybe," Bennett said. "Or maybe, when Doc goes in for one of his famously long appointments, we can go to his laboratory and look at this under his big old microscope."

"You're going to get me fired, Ben."

"He wouldn't do that to you. You're his prized future veterinarian. He's teaching you everything he knows and he even says that you'll own this animal hospital someday."

"Your mother was right," Natalie said. "Laird men are completely unreasonable."

Bennett hid in the back room until Doctor Monaco went into one of the exam rooms for his next appointment. When Natalie signaled him, they tiptoed down the hall and uncovered Doc's vintage Karl Zeiss microscope.

"Let me do this," Natalie said, turning on the light and aligning the dot under the low power lens and then setting the magnification higher. "What are you trying to prove, anyway?"

"Mom and Dad get to have adventures and solve mysteries all the time. Now it's my turn. What do you see in there?"

"Keep your voice down," Natalie said. "I can't see anything. There's writing maybe, but it's too small."

"Let me look."

That was when the door to the exam room opened.

"Crap," Ben said, as he grabbed the snapshot and his textbook and stepped behind a large stainless-steel cabinet with glass doors.

Natalie pretended to be cleaning the lab when Doctor Dominic Monaco came down the hall. He was a strong, lanky man who wore a black patch over his left eye ever since—as the story was oft told—he'd been kicked in the head by a horse, years earlier. Those who understood the doctor's boundless enthusiasm and mischievous sense of humor agreed that the horse story may or may not be true, but none doubted his generosity and love of animals.

"Natalie, are you done feeding the boarders already?"

"No, Doc, I'll get right back to that."

"You do that," Doc said. "And why is Bennett Laird hiding behind the drug cabinet?"

"I'm sorry, Doc," Natalie said.

"Do you want me to neuter your boyfriend like a German shepherd?"

"Definitely not," Natalie said. "He just had a chemistry question."

"Then get out of here, you damn mouse," Doc Monaco said as he ushered Bennett to the back door. "Come back later when I don't have clients waiting and Natalie is done with her work, and we'll talk about chemistry all you want."

Little Havana

Lorraine Calhoun Laird took a flight from Providence to Miami that afternoon with her Leica camera, her reporter's notebook, and clothes for an overnight stay in the semi-tropical city. She wore a wide-brimmed hat for protection from the sun, since tanning made the faded white scar on her left temple more obvious.

"How was your flight?" Connor said when he and Ali met her curbside at Miami International Airport.

"It felt like an escape," Lorraine said. "It was thirty-seven degrees and raining in Rhode Island this morning."

"Got to love that change in latitude," Ali said.

"How was your meeting with Rene Garcia?"

"Fine," Connor said. "We're in the clear."

"But he knows that we're still pursuing this thing," Lorraine said, "doesn't he?"

"Right," Connor said. "Garcia hasn't given up the ship either, even if the politicos would prefer not to lift the scab off an old Cold War wound. But he agrees that we're poking at something a lot bigger just below the surface, so we better have concrete proof before we accuse the Russians of some evil deeds on American soil."

Ali said, "What could be bigger than attempting to murder my parents, kidnapping me as an infant, and trying to kill an airliner full of passengers to get rid of the evidence?"

"Right," Connor said. "But as bad as all that is, there's got to be more to this."

They were a few minutes late when they arrived at the restaurant in Little Havana where they were to meet the lawyers, and their rental car looked out of place in the line of Bentleys, Mercedes-Benz, and Land Rovers at the valet parking.

"We might be a little underdressed for this place," Ali said, since the pilots were still dressed in the casual civilian clothes they had worn for their simulator session, although Connor had put on a blue blazer over his chinos and polo shirt.

"You're fine," Lorraine said.

"I guess so," Ali said. "But what do I say to Vicente's children when I meet them for the first time? Their father died protecting me in a shootout."

"Just tell them how much you appreciate their father's work in trying to find Pilar," Lorraine said.

"Right," Connor said. "And ask them to pick up where Vicente left off by helping you get your family fortune out of that Swiss bank."

"That must be Angela and Bernardo," Lorraine said when they went inside and the maître d' directed them. "But who is that gent seated with them?"

"I'll be darned," Connor said. "That old hombre is Paco, Vicente Molina's best friend and right-hand man. He decided to live in Puerto Rico after Cuba went to the Commies and still refuses to speak English. I wonder how they got him to come north?"

"So, you've met him?"

"Not exactly," Ali whispered. "That old man stalked me in San Juan. The sight of him scared the crap out of me when Vicente lured us into his den of thieves for our first meeting."

"Relax," Connor said. "Paco is one of the good guys."

Vicente's daughter and son stood at their table when the trio approached.

"Welcome to Miami," Angela Molina said. She was a refined and well-dressed woman of middle age and obviously a very successful professional.

"We're sorry for your loss," Lorraine said. "Vicente was a wonderful man."

"Yes," Ali said. "I'll always be grateful for his kindness and courage."

"Thank you," Angela said. "That's very kind. This is my brother, Bernardo."

"Pleased to meet you," Bernardo said. He was a tall young man in a magnificent dark suit with every hair in place.

"And this is my father's dear friend, Fernando Castro," Angela said. "Father called him Paco."

"Yes, we've met," Ali said.

"*Buenas tardes, amigo*," Connor said to Paco as they sat.

They ordered dinner before their words turned to business. Chicken for Lorraine and Ali, and seafood for Connor. Then Angela Molina dropped the bad news on Ali.

"Unfortunately," Angela said, "as far as legal matters go, there's not much we can do for you. Our father could not give up the old animosities, but our law practice is now concerned with the future, not the past. It simply wouldn't be appropriate for us to represent you."

"I'm sorry to hear that," Ali said. "Vicente was my best hope for finding my family in Cuba. I had expected that you would continue his work."

"Ali, we have a heavy load of business law to focus on, mostly contracts and real estate. We couldn't possibly allocate our firm's resources to other matters."

"Quite frankly," Ali said, "that sucks."

With a slight smile, Bernardo chose that moment to enter the conversation.

"If you would allow me," he said to Ali, "Paco has something he would like to say to you. As you know he does not speak English, but I would be happy to translate his words."

"Please do," Ali said.

The old hombre looked at Ali as he spoke slowly in a rasping voice, in a duet with Bernardo's smooth baritone translation.

"*Conoci a tu madre muy bien. Ella fue una inspiracion.*"

"I knew your mother very well. She was an inspiration."

"*Los palabras de Fidel fueron hermosas mentiras.*"

"Fidel's words were beautiful lies."

The dual narrative continued, although after a time Ali only heard Bernardo's voice—

"Pilar believed that he would free Cuba from the oppression of Batista ... Her art made the revolution glorious, and Fidel a demigod ... But freedom for Cuba was only a dream. Fidel would never share the wealth and power ... He murdered all who would oppose his total control. Thousands died ... His passion plunged Cuba into darkness and poverty where no man can be free ... This was when Pilar was painting her heroic portrait of Fidel against a blue sky, a magnificent image ... But on the day of the unveiling Pilar exposed a grotesque portrait that showed hundreds of mutilated corpses around Fidel ... In one stroke she exposed her former hero as a murderous dictator for all to see ... Fidel himself led the soldiers when they came to arrest Pilar and destroy the image..."

"*Pilar nunca mas fue vista.*"

"Pilar was never seen again."

"*Su nombre no debia ser hablado.*"

"Her name was not to be spoken."

"*Estas cosas que he visto con mis propios ojos.*"

"These things I have seen with my own eyes."

Then Paco calmly went back to eating his meal and for a brief time there was only silence at the table.

"So, there it is," Angela Molina finally said. "Given that Pilar was such a high-profile figure in the revolution, we should defer to a law firm specializing in those matters. However, you will find many attorneys in Miami who would welcome this case."

"What you're implying," Lorraine said, "is that your well-heeled Cuban clients here in Miami wouldn't take kindly to your representing someone who once held close ties to Fidel Castro, and finally turned against him when he found communism."

"That's the problem with changing horses in midstream," Connor said. "Both sides tend to hate you."

"Whatever Pilar Vasquez's true sympathies might have been," Angela said, "her estate and her possible marriage to Ernesto Fuentes are bound by Cuban law, which neither Bernardo or I are trained in."

"In other words," Lorraine said, "you don't want to tackle a high-profile case that you might very well lose in the end."

Ali said, "I thought that every person was entitled to the best possible representation."

"I'm sorry," Angela said. "I have to look after the interests of the firm, and this matter is simply too volatile, especially considering that Ernesto Fuentes was a notorious drug smuggler."

Ali was speechless. Lorraine put a comforting hand on her shoulder.

Then Bernardo said, "I'm not so sure about that. I don't see the harm in helping Miss Vasquez determine the fate of her family and possibly even recover her inheritance. Perhaps we could look through our father's notes to determine the facts surrounding her claim and contact Credit Suisse on her behalf. It could all be handled very discreetly."

"What my baby brother means to say," Angela said, with a restraining hand on Bernardo's forearm, "is that we just don't want to go down that road. Our practice would then be open to many conflicts of interest."

It startled all of them around the table when Paco said in perfect English, "Vicente would want you to do right by Senorita Vasquez."

"Ha!" Bernardo said after the moment of surprise passed. "That settles it. Come to the office tomorrow and we'll draw up an agreement. There will be no fee unless we are successful, of course."

Nightfall

"What do you expect from Bernardo tomorrow?" Lorraine said this to Ali after they settled into their corner suite of rooms on the fourteenth floor of the Intercontinental Hotel, where the two women sipped glasses of wine and looked over the skyline of Miami, drenched in the vibrant colors of a tropical sunset.

"I have a good feeling about him," Ali said.

"Yes," Lorraine said. "I noticed."

"You have to admit, he is dreamy."

"He's a dandy," Connor said, taking a seat next to Lorraine on the sofa with a glass of cranberry juice. "But Angela is calling all the shots in their shop."

"Did you notice his wristwatch?" Lorraine said. "That was a Patek Phillippe, which makes a Rolex look like a dime-store item."

"Just like the one your father used to wear," Connor said.

"The high-end accoutrements were only part of Bertram's *shtick* with the Foreign Service," Lorraine said. "He had to look and act the part when speaking for the wealthiest nation on Earth. These days he prefers chinos and old sweaters."

"Maybe Bernardo has an image to uphold," Ali said.

"Maybe he just likes bling," Connor said.

"Well," Lorraine said, "there's no doubt that the Molina law firm is highly profitable. Some people familiar with the Miami business scene describe it as a goldmine."

"Right," Connor said to Ali. "I think that Bernardo did the calculus of your potential inheritance to his fees and decided you were too good a deal to pass up."

"Then again," Lorraine said, "he might want to carry on where his father left off. We know that Vicente Molina started out as a freedom fighter with a gun but turned to the law to help ordinary people get some measure of justice from the Cuban government. Perhaps Bernardo can do the same."

"That would be very nice," Ali said.

"Anyway," Connor said as he stood up. "I'm going to call Ben before I hit the sack. But you ought to read this agreement Bernardo is drawing up very carefully."

"I'd also say to be careful around Bernardo," Lorraine told Ali, after Connor left them. "Remember, he's your lawyer, not your new interest."

"Is it that obvious?"

"Yes. And I can't say I blame you because he is a gorgeous man. But there is a lot about Bernardo that you don't know."

"I know that he was not wearing a wedding ring."

"Right. So how does a wealthy attorney remain single? He might be the fastest playboy in Miami."

"That's okay." Ali smiled mischievously over her wineglass. "I'm not smitten. But I wouldn't mind getting to know Bernardo Molina."

CHAPTER

2

Thursday, March 17, 2005

Dawn Patrol

The morning was cold and dismal on the coast of Rhode Island with an inch of mushy snow on the ground, but Bennett already had his wetsuit on when he and Natalie drove to Easton's Beach with his surfboard on the roof and the old German shepherd in the backseat.

"Surf's up," Natalie said when Bennett nosed his Jeep up to the seawall.

"It looks a little sloppy," he said after they got out and stood on the concrete wall above the sand. "But it'll work."

The shepherd sniffed around underfoot while Bennett got his surfboard off the Jeep's roof. Then the boy put on the hood of his wetsuit and pulled the collar open so that Natalie could pour a thermos of warm water down the front. She had to hold the dog's collar when Bennett ran down to the water with his board.

"Stay with me, Fenway," she said. "It's too cold for you in the water today."

Then Natalie sat with the dog and took a handwritten poem out of her pocket and read it again while Bennett paddled out prone through spilling surf.

Mornings are bleak
School, the games people play
Until I hear you speak
Then, I have a good day
Until sleep comes and I smile
Thinking only of you

Bennett took the icy whitewater in his face with a laugh and looked for the places on the long curving surf-line where the gray waves were curling. He knew everyone sitting on their boards beyond the breakers and waiting for the right wave when he padded into the circle and said, "What's up, dudes?"

"Not much here," one of the men said. "The action is all over at Ruggles today."

"I see that," Bennett said, looking out to the rocky point of land where the mansions of the Gilded Era stood along Bellevue Avenue with their backs to the sea. "We ought to be over there with the ripe waves."

"I don't know," the man said. "It looks pretty crowded already."

"Those guys are assholes," another surfer said. "They'll knock you off your board and mess you up if you drop in on their break."

"Or they'll key the paint and slash the tires on your car," another said. "It's just not worth it."

"Nobody owns the waves," Bennett said. "I think I'll just go over and take a look."

He left the group by stroking hard to catch the rolling water of an average little wave—only two feet tall—and jumped to his feet when he was lifted by the energy of the sea, which rose up to meet his board and held him suspended for a brief moment in time.

All too soon he carved the board to a stop and leapt off into the knee-deep water of the receding wash, where he carried his board back to the Jeep.

"Had enough already?" Natalie said, handing him a towel after he pulled off his hood and peeled the top of his wetsuit off.

"Let's go check out the action on Ruggles Avenue," Bennett said as he shrugged into his hooded sweatshirt.

"You're crazy," Natalie said. "You'd better show up with a posse if you want to tangle with that crowd."

"You're my posse," Bennett said, laughing as they drove past the Forty Steps and Ochre Court, and behind the grand architecture of Chateau-sur-Mer and Fredrick Law Olmstead Park, all devoid of tourists on the raw day. He parked near the end of Ruggles Avenue close to the wall around the Vanderbilts' marble mansion—aptly named The Breakers—for behind it some of the largest and most dramatic surf in New England could be found crashing on the rocks of Ochre Point.

"Let's go down to Cliff Walk and take a look," Bennett said.

Waves were building over the shoals along the Cliff Walk and spilling onto the rocks in wild, churning wash. Some of the old guys who had laid claim to the surf there were walking on the path toward the water, and they greeted Bennett and Natalie with apparent disdain when they came down the steps from Ruggles Avenue.

"Shouldn't you be in school?"

"It's a snow day," Bennett said. "And it's Saint Patrick's Day. Shouldn't you be on a barstool?"

"Watch your mouth, kid."

"What's with the wetsuit, kid?" a grizzled old surfer said. "You'd better not try dropping in on our break."

"Your break? You don't even live in Newport. You drive down from Boston to surf in my backyard."

"Listen, kid," said another man with a three-day-old beard and a longboard under his arm. "We've been coming here since before you were born, so get lost."

"I don't think so," Bennett said.

"Watch all you want," another man said. "But this is no place for a grommet like you. You'll wipe out, and I'm not going to risk my ass saving you."

"Maybe I'll save you," Bennett said.

The older surfers laughed and kept walking along Cliff Walk with their boards, but a tall young man stopped to face Bennett.

"You're the runner, right? Nate Laird's kid brother?"

"Yup. I know you, too. You're Jeremy Croft. Some people say you're the best distance runner ever at Rogers High School, and I'm the kid who's going to break your record in the mile run."

"Ha! Good luck with that."

"We've got a good team this year."

Jeremy patted Bennett on the head as he walked by, and said, "You'd better open up that stride, Shorty."

Which would have really pissed Bennett off—especially since Natalie was right there—except that the slightly older surfer turned around and spoke as he walked away.

"Listen, these guys aren't so tough," Jeremy said. "Be out here at first light some morning when the surf isn't too big and maybe I'll go out with you."

"Awesome."

"First light, no later."

"Deal," Bennett said, as he and Natalie walked back to his Jeep.

"Listen," Natalie said, "you don't have to drop in at Ruggles."

"Why not?"

"It's too dangerous, Ben. There are too many rocks and the waves are unpredictable. I don't want you to do it."

"Don't worry. If they can do it, I can do it."

They were driving up Bellevue Avenue when she said, "Why do you have to be so reckless? You're a madman on your motocross bike and when we go scuba diving you always want to go too deep. Now you want to surf the biggest waves in New England. What are you trying to prove?"

"I'm just having a little fun."

"No, you're hiding yourself, Ben. You don't want anyone to know how sensitive you really are. You write beautiful poems for me that nobody else ever sees. I've saved them all, you know. Someday I'll put them in a book so everybody can read them."

"You wouldn't do that. Nobody would believe a knucklehead like me writes poetry. They'll think you wrote them to yourself."

When Bennett parked his Jeep behind the hedges that separated the Laird house from Catherine Street, they saw that smoke was rising from the chimney above the living room, signaling that Bertram had stoked the fireplace there.

Natalie said, "Is your grandfather staying here permanently?"

"I don't know why he would," Bennett said. "He has a big brick mansion and lots of friends in Charleston."

"Maybe he's lonely since your grandmother passed away."

Bennett had stripped off his wetsuit bottoms and put on sweatpants to match his hoodie before they left Ruggles, so he was mostly dry and almost warm when they went into the kitchen. Fenway trotted through the house, sniffing around to see if anything had changed while they were out, and Bennett went straight to the refrigerator for a half gallon of milk—but he froze when he looked at the countertop nearest the back door.

"Crap," he said, whispering and pulling on Natalie's arm. "My chemistry book is gone."

"What?"

"It was right here," he said, touching the empty spot on the kitchen countertop.

"Why did you leave it out?"

"I don't know." He shrugged. "But we better find it quick because that picture with the microdot is still in it."

Bennett inched sideways and craned his neck to look around the corner into the living room where he saw his grandfather sitting in his favorite armchair, holding a heavy book and rubbing his short gray whiskers.

"Jeez," Bennett pulled back and whispered to Natalie. "I can't get a break around here."

"You made your own bad break by leaving that book out with the picture still in it."

"Thanks a lot, Nattie. But why would Bertram be reading a chemistry textbook? He already knows everything."

"Follow me," Natalie said, smiling mischievously.

"Hi, Ambassador," she said after rounding the corner into the living room. "That's a nice fire you've made."

"It certainly is," Bertram said. "Come sit by the hearth and warm up, Bennett. You must be half-frozen. Why would you want to go surfing in winter weather?"

"That's when the big waves come our way," Bennett said, avoiding eye contact. "It's mostly flat around here in the summer."

The ambassador looked the part of an outdoorsman and senior statesman in the leather armchair, resplendent in a heavy Nordic sweater.

"Okay," Natalie said, with a big smile. "We're going to go upstairs to study now."

"Brilliant!" Bertram said. "Why don't you two remain here and do your work. I might even be of some assistance."

"Nope." Bennett shrugged. "Our school stuff is all upstairs."

"I see," Bertram said, holding up the textbook. "Then won't you require this?"

"Oh, I guess so," Bennett said, trying to look nonchalant when he accepted the book. "Thanks, Grandpa."

"You're most welcome." Then Bertram had the picture in his hand when he said, "Now would you care to explain how you came to possess this item?"

"Uh—I—" Bennett stammered. "I guess I should have told you about that."

"Young man, you are the master of understatement. Who else knows of this?"

"Just me and Nattie," Bennett said. "Sorry, Grandpa. I picked it up after Ransom punched out the Russian. I was going to give it to Dad after I read the secret message."

"That was foolish of you," Bertram said, pointing a weathered finger at his grandson. "You are exposed to criminal prosecution for withholding evidence and interfering with a federal investigation. The enormity of your ignorance will be no defense."

"Sorry, Grandpa."

"I'm guilty, too," Natalie said.

"I won't condemn you for attempting to mislead me, Miss Natalie," Bertram said. "Not this one time. I suspect that your devotion to Bennett compels you to extricate him from difficulty in a manner that you would not employ on your own behalf."

"Yes, sir," Natalie said.

"Very well then," Bertram said, turning back to Bennett. "Get dressed, young man. We're on a mission."

"We have to turn the picture over to the FBI, don't we?"

"Not so fast." Bertram held up his hand. "I'm not above the law, but my status as ambassador-at-large does grant me a certain latitude in matters of state. We'll take your Jeep."

Natalie said, "Can I come?"

"Of course, you can. You're part of the family."

Natalie followed Bennett upstairs to his room, but the German shepherd stayed behind and settled on the floor near Bertram's feet and the fire.

"What was that Bertram said?" Bennett said, when he stripped down to his baggy swim trunks. "Something about you doing stuff to get me out of trouble?"

Natalie rifled through Ben's drawers, selecting some clothes for him to wear.

"He said I'd lie for you when I wouldn't lie for myself."

"Yup," Bennett said, pointing both thumbs at himself with a laugh. "And you're devoted to this guy, right?"

"Shut up, ass-hat." Natalie shoved the stack of folded clothes hard against Bennett's chest. "I'll be downstairs with the ambassador."

Bernardo

"Should we call Bernardo's law office and get an appointment for this morning?"

Ali Vasquez asked the question while they were having breakfast in their suite at the Intercontinental Hotel.

"He didn't say a time," Connor said, "so you could just show up whenever."

"Connor has a point," Lorraine said. "I have a feeling that Bernardo will see you as soon as you come in the door. The office is only three blocks away so we could walk over."

"Great," Connor said. "While you gals are doing that, I'll take the rental car down to Key Biscayne and look at boats."

"What?" Ali said. "You're not coming with us?"

"It's been fun, Ali, but my part in this caper is all over. You and Lorraine can take it from here."

"I might still need your help," Ali said.

"Doing what? Lorraine is doing the research and writing the book, and the lawyers are going to recover your inheritance. So you don't need me to wrap this up."

"I'd feel better having you around," Lorraine said. "Just in case."

"Relax, Peaches. We really did a number on those guys. They're all dead or in jail, so they won't be causing trouble."

"Except for Nick Volkov."

"We kicked his ass all the way back to Mother Russia," Connor said. "The Kremlin is probably over it by now."

"Except that the FBI never found the picture of Ernesto," Ali said. "Aren't you worried that Volkov's comrades might come looking for the microdot if they suspect we still have it?"

"Ali is right," Lorraine said. "We should all be concerned that some bad actors may still be on the loose."

"Okay," Connor said. "I'll go with you guys even though I've had more than my fill of lawyers lately."

"Good," Lorraine said. "And you're bringing your gun, right?"

"Sure," Connor said, going to his suitcase to get the pistol. "If it makes you feel better."

The morning was warm and pleasant when they walked over to the Molina Law Office on Castro Street, which was housed in a modern building owned by the firm.

"You were certainly right about not needing an appointment," Ali said when the trio was ushered into a conference room as soon as they arrived.

"Nice digs," Connor said, admiring the long mahogany table that dominated the room. "Their rates must be astronomical to pay for this setup."

"Sure," Lorraine said, walking around the room and looking at the model race cars and powerboats on a side table. "It looks like Bernardo has some big boys' toys and a need for speed."

"Hey, guys," Ali said, waving them over. "Check out this portrait of Vicente."

They gathered at the painting overlooking the conference table bearing the countenance and name of Jose Vicente Molina Carminates in a double-breasted suit with wide lapels and his powerful right hand on a stack of law books.

"This is a great likeness of him," Ali said.

"It is," Lorraine said. "He was one tough old bull."

"Right," Connor muttered as aides circulated through the room, bringing files and coffee to the table. "We'll see what Little Bernardo brings."

Connor's words were still hanging in the air a moment later when the aides stopped what they were doing and turned to face attorney Bernardo Molina when he came into the room.

"Alicia!" Bernardo said, walking straight to her and offering his hand. "I'm delighted that you have come this morning."

"I hope you don't mind that I brought Lorraine and Connor," Ali said.

"Of course," he said, taking their hands in turn while flashing a boyish smile that even Connor would later admit was quite charming. With perfect teeth, a light blue silk shirt open at the collar, and a trim waistline, he might have been the young prince ruling the kingdom with relaxed grace—as long as his older sister was not around.

"I like to get to business first," Bernardo said, after they were seated at the table. "Here is a copy of an agreement I'd like to offer to you. Let's read it together."

The young lawyer read the contract in a very clear voice, ensuring that Ali understood the legalese without a hint of condescension. She hung on his every word and when he was finished she said, "That sounds good to me."

"Very well," Bernardo said. "Although there will be no fees unless we are successful, this is not a *pro bono* arrangement so we usually ask for a small retainer to seal the contract. Say, ten thousand dollars?"

"I haven't got it," Ali said, even though she still carried an envelope stuffed with C-notes.

"We can loan you whatever you require," Lorraine offered.

"No, please," Bernardo said, raising a manicured hand a few inches off the table. "What amount would you be comfortable with, Alicia?"

"I suppose I could come up with one thousand."

"That will be quite satisfactory," Bernardo said, entering the amount in the blank on the agreement.

"I must admit that I am at a bit of a loss," Bernardo said, as he pushed the signed papers aside. "My father kept me far away from matters concerning Cuba. But luckily, I have his friend Fredrico Castro, whom you met last night, to fill in the gaps in my knowledge."

"And you must have access to Vicente's notes?" Lorraine said.

"Oh yes, I've read parts of the file. My father kept boxes of documents from this case under lock and key, so it will take weeks to go through it all. But I've read enough to know that the houses of Vasquez and Fuentes were joined by marriage in the generation preceding Pilar and Ernesto and that when a romantic relationship developed between the teenagers, young Ernesto Fuentes was sent to live in the Sierra Maestra with his mother's brother, Ernesto Vasquez."

"That's what I've been told," Ali said. "Pilar and Ernesto were first cousins."

"Which is a problem," Bernardo said. "Cuban law would never allow first cousins to marry, so it may be difficult to prove that Ernesto was your father."

"He and Pilar lived in the Sierra Maestra for months before they fled to America," Ali said. "He has to be my father."

"Yes, but that's the bigger problem," Bernardo said. "According to the Cuban courts Pilar Vasquez died of natural causes in the *Presidio Modelo* on March 16, 1972, after which her remains were entombed in the family crypt at the *Cemrenterio Christobal Colon* in Havana. She was thirty-three years old."

"None of us believes that," Lorraine said. "We've found the wreck of Ernesto's airplane in the Everglades and there's plenty of evidence that Pilar and Ali were aboard when it crashed."

"Which from a legal point of view only compounds the problem," Bernardo said. "Ali's forged adoption certificate lists her place of birth as

Immokalee, Florida. So it will be extremely difficult to prove that she was born to Pilar and Ernesto in Cuba."

"None of that really matters to me," Ali said. "I just want to find Pilar."

"You believe that she may still be alive?" Bernardo said.

"Pilar would only be sixty-six years old," Lorraine said. "If she survived the crash."

"Is that possible?"

"Sure," Connor said. "When we looked at the wreck, there was a passenger seat facing aft in the rear of the cabin. Someone sitting there almost certainly would have survived if they got out of the airplane before the fire."

"Very well," Bernardo said. "The first rule in a case like this is to follow the money, so I will contact my father's friend in Zurich. Herr Rochat was investigating the existence of a Vasquez family account at Credit Suisse and he may have very valuable information for us."

"That's great," Ali said. "Thank you."

"Ah," Bernardo said, raising a hand. "There is much more. My father had identified an account in the Bank of Israel that had been opened by Ernesto Fuentes's uncle, Ernesto Vasquez, when he was a principle in an airline named Intercontinental Aerea de Cuba."

"Sure," Connor said. "That outfit was put together by some Cuban flyboys to transport Jews in the Exodus. They did some hairy flying over hostile Arab territory in surplus Curtiss C-46 transports to bring refugees from Iran and Yemen."

"That's correct," Bernardo said. "The airline was based in Havana, but most business was conducted through Nicosia, Cyprus. The elder Ernesto was already a millionaire, so he deposited all the money he made from that venture in the nascent Bank of Israel to bolster their holdings. Much of it remains there drawing compound interest."

"I'm not surprised the old ace did that," Connor said. "He was a great old-time pilot and two-time world aerobatic champion. I see a lot of him in Ali."

"That's interesting," Bernardo said, "because the elder Ernesto bequeathed all his worldly possessions to his nephew."

"So that money in Israel might go to Ali?" Lorraine said.

"Yes and no," Bernardo said. "Even if we can establish that Ernesto was Ali's father, there is a complication."

"What's that?" Ali said.

"You are probably not aware that the younger Ernesto had a family in Argentina," Bernardo said. "He married there after fleeing the revolution but left his wife and children in Buenos Aires to return to Cuba in order to fly Pilar to freedom."

"Oh my God," Ali said. "Children? I had no idea."

"Quite true," Bernardo said. "We know this because his daughter has been waging a legal battle to withdraw the funds from Israel for several years now. You may even recognize the name—Ernesto Fuentes's daughter is Sofia Fuentes Lavallee."

"Never heard of her," Ali said.

"The designer?" Lorraine said. "Ernesto's daughter is the fashion maven Sofia Lavallee?"

"Correct," Bernardo said.

"No wonder I never heard of her," Ali said, with a thin smile. "I buy my clothes off the rack. So where can I find her?"

"Sofia has studios in London and Dubai," Bernardo said. "I believe that she is working out of London at this time."

"Good," Ali said, standing up. "In that case I'm on my way to merry old London-town."

"That might not be wise," Bernardo said. "Perhaps I should contact her studio with a letter explaining your situation beforehand."

"Bernardo is right," Lorraine said. "Sofia is famously difficult."

"I don't care," Ali said. "It isn't even about the money. I have to find out if I have a half-sister."

"I could arrange for an attorney in London to contact Sofia," Bernardo said. "I fear that walking in unannounced might not end well."

"No worries," Ali said, extending her hand to Bernardo. "You keep working on the legal angle. I've got this part."

School of War

"Where to?" Bennett said to his grandfather when they climbed into his Jeep. He still had his surfboard on the roof and Natalie had to push his soggy wetsuit aside to take the backseat.

"The Navy Base at Coaster's Harbor," Bertram said. "Does this vehicle have heat?"

"It takes a minute to warm up, Grandpa."

"Let's hope it is a short minute," Bertram said. "I'm continually amazed by your immunity to cold, like your surfing on a winter morning. What is it that calls you into freezing water?"

"I don't know. I guess I like the waves."

Natalie leaned forward as Bennett drove past the Touro Synagogue on Bellevue Avenue and said, "Tell him what you told me, Ben,"

"I don't think so." Bennett shrugged. "I was just being goofy, Nattie."

"No, you weren't. Tell your grandfather what surfing feels like. Remember? The energy?"

"This I have to hear," Bertram said, twisting in his seat to get a better view of his grandson, who was then navigating his Jeep through the narrow colonial streets and Quaker homes of Newport's Point district.

"Well, it's just that when you're up on a wave you're falling—you're coming down the wave but the wave is building underneath you too, pushing you up. It's like you're a satellite in orbit around the Earth, always falling but never coming down."

"Yes," Bertram said. "In fact, I do understand and that is a grand thought, Bennett."

When they crossed the low bridge to Coasters Island, the gate guard at the Navy Base hesitated to allow Bennett's dilapidated Jeep pass until Bertram produced his State Department credentials, which drew a snappy salute.

"Are we going to the O-Club for lunch?" Bennett said as he drove onto the base.

"Not today," Bertram said. "Carry on to the Naval War College, directly ahead."

"Park there," Bertram said when they were in front of Connolly Hall, the largest and most modern building on the campus.

"But, Grandpa, that sign says the spot is reserved for admirals."

"An ambassador-at-large is the equivalent of a four-star admiral for military honors, Bennett."

"Cool."

Inside, Bertram steered Bennett away from the areas where the computerized war games were staged and turned instead to the polished hallways that led into the academic section, where they stopped at the door to an office marked *Dr. Sergei Mikhailov, HUMINT*.

"Sergei?" Bennett asked before the trio went in. "Isn't that a Russian name?"

"Certainly," Bertram said.

Natalie asked, "What is HUMINT?"

"Human intelligence," Bertram said. "Who better to teach our senior naval officers about the methodology of Russian spies than a former KGB man?"

"But he's on our side now?" Bennett said. "Right?"

"Listen," Bertram said, whispering and putting his hand on Natalie's shoulder. "In this business there are only two people I trust, me and Natalie. And I'm not so sure about Natalie."

"Very funny," Bennett said.

"That's an old joke, Bennett, with a loaded message. Talk to this man, but be certain not to mention any names, places, or dates. When it comes to this item, let me do the talking."

"Got it," Bennett said.

Professor Mikhailov, a short, slightly portly man with unkempt gray hair, was watering a plant in the window when he bade them to enter his office. There were what appeared to be mundane items on the shelves of his space—cameras, portable radios, a typewriter-like device, and a framed World War Two poster reminding that *Loose Lips Sink Ships*.

"Ah, Ambassador Calhoun, please come in," Sergei said, the words heavily accented. "It is an honor to have you in my humble office."

"Thank you for seeing me today," Bertram said. "As I mentioned on the telephone I've brought some young people to see you. This is my grandson Bennett and his friend Natalie."

It took Bennett three tries to get Doctor Mikhailov's name almost right, but when he pronounced it close enough for the introductions, the trio took chairs around his desk.

"So, Ambassador Calhoun, what can I do for you today?"

"These young people have an interest in your tradecraft, Professor."

"I see," Sergei said, smiling at Bennett. "Young man, why would you believe that I have any knowledge of such matters?"

"Didn't you used to be in the KGB?"

"Perhaps. Do you know what those letters stand for? That was the *Komitet Gosudarstvennoy Bezopasnosti*, the Committee for State Security for the Soviet Union."

"I could never pronounce that name," Bennett said.

"Then you might have some trouble with the current security service of the Russian Federation, *Glavnoye Razvedyvatel'noye Upravleniye*, which we call the GRU."

"Those names are really different," Bennett said.

"I have a question," Natalie said. "If you don't mind me asking, why did you come to America? Weren't we the enemy of the KGB?"

"Quite frankly," Sergei said, leaning back in his chair, "when the Soviet Union ceased to exist, I could no longer make a decent living in Russia."

"There were no jobs for you?"

"I am educated as a nuclear physicist but so are a million others, more than could ever work in that field. Yet if the Committee for State Security still existed, I might be a very wealthy man."

"You mean that in Russia," Bennett said, "spies get paid more than scientists?"

"Yes, decidedly so. State secrets and the capacity for violence were the primary currency of the Soviet system. The goal of every KGB agent was to become a wealthy man in a system with no clear distinction between government and organized crime."

"That doesn't sound very nice," Natalie said.

"It was very, very nice for those State Security men who became the oligarchs," Sergei said. "They are now the wealthiest men in Russia."

"But isn't spying all done by computers now?" Bennett said.

"That is profoundly untrue," Sergei said. "Human intelligence gathering will always be the most effective method of gaining an advantage over an adversary. You see, it is often more conversational than clandestine. A well-trained operative can identify and exploit the weaknesses of any individual by appearing to be a friend with access to money, drugs, or forbidden sex. The target will be eager to become an asset and relay information to the operative, like harmless gossip. It becomes an excitement, like a gambler entering a casino, or an alcoholic approaching a bar."

"I can't believe they teach that stuff here," Bennett said.

"Quite to the contrary," Sergei said, with a chuckle. "The only way to defend against an adversary is to know their methods. I teach countermeasures and a general history course of our tradecraft from Roman times to Al-Qaeda's current techniques for radicalizing converts."

Then the retired spy turned to Bertram and said, "So what brings you to me today?"

"You have some interesting devices in your office," Bertram said when Bennett and Natalie looked his way.

"Ah, yes," Sergei said, waving his hand at the displays. "All the tools of the trade. That is an Enigma decoding machine, a rare four-rotor version used by the *Wehrmacht*. The cribbage board is a crystal radio of the type smuggled into POW camps in Red Cross packages, and that alarm clock contains a miniature reel-to-reel tape recorder once used by the East German *Stasi*."

"A very impressive collection," Bertram said. "What can you tell us about microdots?"

"They have been used to convey secret messages since the Franco-Prussian War," Sergei said. "In fact, many equipment manufacturers still place them on their high-value devices to aid in identification. Would you like to see one?"

"That would be splendid," Bertram said.

"I use this device for my classes," Sergei said, taking a microscope off the shelf. "If you come over to the window for the light, you may find it interesting."

"Wow," Bennett said when he took a turn looking into the microscope. "That's the Gettysburg Address on a tiny dot."

"Brilliant!" Bertram said, reaching into his coat pocket. "Might you read this one?"

The ambassador handed the picture of young Ernesto Fuentes to Sergei, who produced a magnifying glass from his desk to study it.

"Very interesting," Sergei said. "The dot affixed to this snapshot is an advanced type, as you may already know. May I ask how you came to possess this rare example, Ambassador?"

"A friend found that in some family papers," Bertram said. "We were unable to read it under a laboratory microscope."

"Yes, reading this will require some special equipment, which I just happen to have."

Sergei went to the storage closet and wheeled out a small table with a tall white tube-like device.

"This happens to be one of the few combination camera-readers of this type to be found outside of Russia," he said, as he put a small tray with a sample dot into the device. "Take a look."

"That's the whole Declaration of Independence," Natalie said, when given a turn at the eyepiece.

"Yes," Sergei said, "including the signatures of the signers. Even John Hancock."

"So, we could read our microdot with this device?" Bertram said.

"Yes, but I would have to remove the dot from the photograph and there is always a small chance that it might be damaged by doing so."

"I believe we'll take that chance if you are willing to give it a try."

Sergei sat down and used a scalpel to carefully remove the dot from Ali's snapshot of Ernesto, then put it in a small tray to be inserted into the tube.

"This is quite remarkable," Sergei said as he looked in the eyepiece and adjusted the device. "Where did you say this came from?"

"It came from a friend," Bertram said. "May I have a look?" Looking in the eyepiece, the ambassador said, "Brilliant!"

"What is it?" Bennett said, with a need to know.

"Take a look," Bertram said.

"Darn it," Bennett said. "It's just numbers. I hate numbers."

"It's a code," Natalie said, when she had her turn to look.

"Quite correct," Bertram said. "Military and diplomatic messages are often sent as groups of numbers that can only be deciphered by specialists with the requisite equipment."

"No," Sergei said. "This is not just any code. I recognize these groups of numbers. This is a special cypher that was only used for a few years after the Cuban Missile Crisis."

"Of course," Bertram said. "The Soviets realized we had cracked their military codes during the crisis. This was their answer, a whole new system. Is that not correct?"

"Regrettably, you are correct, Ambassador. This particular code was only used for a short time in the early '60s, but it is still very sensitive. You should not possess this message."

"Well, that's neither here nor there, Professor. We have it. Can you enlarge and photograph this dot for us?"

"Please, Ambassador. Just take that microdot and leave my office. I want nothing to do with it."

"I realize that this message is probably still highly classified, Professor. But I am an ambassador-at-large and I would very much like to have a photograph of it before I turn it over to the proper authorities."

"I will take that picture for you," Sergei said. "Against my better judgment."

Then the professor of spy craft made some adjustments to the device—removing, turning, and replacing the tray with the microdot in the viewing tube several times.

"The camera mount for this device will only accept a Russian Zenit camera with 35mm film. Can you develop the negatives?"

"Yes," Bertram said. "If we can't use a digital camera, 35mm will have to do."

Sergei loaded the camera with a new roll of film and took several shots through the device. Then he rewound and removed the roll of exposed film and handed it to Bertram along with the microdot, still in the tray he had used in the device.

"Whatever you intend to do with that microdot, please leave my name out of it. I'm in a precarious position here. As a former KGB man, my true faith and allegiance to the United States is sometimes questioned."

"Of course," Bertram said. "Thank you, Professor."

"Thanks, Professor," Bennett said, taking the picture of Ernesto from Sergei's desk as they left his office. "We wouldn't want to forget this."

Then Bennett was the last one of the trio to exit the office and he turned to the professor with one final question on the way out.

"Say, do you know a guy named Nick Volkov? Or maybe Nikoli Volkov?"

"Never heard of him," Professor Mikhailov said. "Have a good day, Bennett."

Reservations

The pilots and Lorraine were back in their suite at the Intercontinental Hotel when Ali put down her phone and said, "That was easy. British Airways has reserved a first-class seat for me on the early flight to London this evening. I just have to bring my airline credentials and pay the tax."

"Then you should get some rest," Lorraine said.

"I'm too wired to sleep. Tomorrow morning, I might be meeting my half-sister for the first time."

"About that," Lorraine said, "shouldn't you call ahead for an appointment? You're not even sure that Sofia is in London right now."

"I doubt she would grant me an audience. My best bet will be walking into her studio unannounced."

"Ali, according to the society magazines, Sofia is notoriously difficult."

"Aren't all designers full of themselves?"

"Not to mention she may not have known Ernesto all that well. I'm guessing she isn't more than ten years older than you, so she would have been very young when he returned to Cuba."

"That doesn't matter. Anything she can tell me puts me that much closer to finding Pilar. Besides, I've seen the wreckage of Ernesto's plane in the Everglades and I can tell her how the CIA and the Russians—and God knows who else—double-crossed our father."

"That should be an interesting conversation," Lorraine said. "Do you need some money?"

"Ha!" Connor said, when he brought his coffee to the sofa where the women were drinking merlot. "Don't worry about Ali. She's still carrying that envelope of cash from Arthur's safe."

"That's true," Ali said, pulling the envelope out of her pocket. "In fact, I've got a bit too much cash on me to go through customs. Would you mind holding on to this envelope until I get back, Connor?"

"You're allowed ten thousand at the border," Connor said. "So you could carry a few grand in case you need it."

"This should be enough," Ali said, pulling a wad of C-notes from her stash before handing the rest to him.

"You really should get a nap before your flight," Lorraine said, watching the envelope change hands. "Connor and I are going to drive up to West Palm Beach this afternoon."

"We are?" Connor said.

"Yes. Bernardo told me about an art dealer in West Palm who may know the whereabouts of some of Pilar's paintings. We can get a flight home out of Fort Lauderdale afterward, can't we?"

"I suppose so," Connor muttered. "Just remember, Nathan is coming home tonight. We ought to be there."

"Then this is good-bye, for now," Ali said when she hugged Lorraine at the door to their suite. "Thank you. I couldn't do this without your help."

"Good luck in London," Lorraine said. "We'll see you when you get back. I'll want to hear about Sofia while it is fresh in your mind."

"What the hell," Ali said, when she turned and embraced Connor. "I guess you get a hug, too."

"Uh, right," Connor said. "Good luck, Vasquez."

West Palm Beach

Lorraine was driving the rental car up the Florida Turnpike when she turned to Connor and said, "How much money is in that envelope?"

"I don't know. Why do you ask?"

"Because neither of you counted it. I don't think Ali even knew exactly how much she took out."

"No big deal." Connor shrugged.

"Still, I wonder," she said. "How close do friends have to be to hand envelopes full of cash to each other, with no counting?"

"We've been through too much to not trust each other, Peaches."

"I suppose," she said. "But I noticed that you held that hug just a bit too long."

"You're jealous?"

"Just tell me, Connor. Now that you and Ali have been cleared by the FAA, are you going to fly trips together again?"

"We might. We'll have to see how the schedule looks next month."

Lorraine pulled the car out of the turnpike traffic into the breakdown lane and stopped short.

"Damn it, Lorraine. Don't stop here. Some drunk will plow into us."

"Connor, this is important. Don't leave me in Rhode Island and fly off to some tropical island with her ever again."

"Nothing is going on. Why can't you accept that?"

"You like flying with her, that's what's going on. You like to teach her everything you know about the airline business and laugh and joke and share secrets with her. And you like to protect her, damn it. I don't want that."

"She's young enough to be my daughter."

"Our daughter," Lorraine said. "Why didn't you say she's young enough to be *our* daughter?"

"Damn it, it's just a figure of speech. Don't make a big deal of it."

"Put her on your no-fly list, Connor. The airline won't put two pilots together if one of them doesn't want to work with the other."

"Twenty-seven thousand hours in the air and I've never put anyone on my no-fly list. I don't want to start now."

Lorraine took a deep breath, but Connor spoke before she could exhale any words.

"Peaches, this isn't the time or the place for this. Let's just get to this gallery, all right?"

She eased the car back into the flow on the turnpike and not much was said for the remainder of the drive to West Palm Beach.

When they arrived at the art dealer recommended by Bernardo, Lorraine parked their economy rental car among the Mercedes and Porsche SUVs in front of the gallery. Inside, they were greeted by Nils Van der Holt, an Afrikaner with a guttural accent and an overtly condescending manner.

"You don't want anything by Pilar Vasquez," the Dutch South African said. "Those paintings are depreciating every day."

"Why do you say that?" Lorraine asked.

"Nobody cares. Vasquez's paintings are no longer relevant. They will soon be worthless."

"Some would say they are now more relevant than ever."

"Bah. Cuba is now a tourist trap, a theme park of the good revolution. I've been there a dozen times myself. Dissident art is passé. Let me show you something by Cundo Bermudez."

"Actually, we're only interested in Vasquez," Lorraine said.

"I'm just going to take a look around," Connor said, breaking away from Lorraine's negotiation with the pedantic art dealer, for whom he had little use.

He wandered aimlessly through the gallery while Lorraine and Nils Van der Holt continued to butt heads across the room and stopped at an abstract painting that might have been done by tossing balloons of paint at the canvas. A boy was down on one knee cleaning the glass of a display case behind where Connor stood, and it took Connor a moment to realize he was talking to him when he spoke.

"To me," the boy said, "that painting looks like an eagle giving birth to a giraffe."

"Right," Connor said, allowing a brief chuckle. On second look the boy was a teenager or a young man. It was hard to tell with his smooth skin and the remnants of baby fat, which soothed his features.

"Pilar Vasquez," the youth said, not looking at Connor. "Her paintings interest you?"

"They do," Connor said, finally deciding that the boy was actually a young man, probably around twenty years old.

"I'll get in trouble if Van der Holt finds out," he said, raising a folded slip of paper toward Connor. "But you can call me later."

When Connor hesitated before taking the scrap of paper from his delicate hand, the young man looked him in the eye for the first time and said, "I might know where you can find a Vasquez painting."

Connor amazed himself when he uttered, "What time do you get off?" in response to the offer.

"I'll be done here in one hour."

"Okay," Connor said.

Lorraine's conversation with the Afrikaner had steadily devolved into a dead end and she was ready to leave the gallery empty-handed. Connor waited until they were outside to show Lorraine the slip of paper.

"I can't believe I took this kid's phone number," he said, after they were back in the rental car.

"What?" Lorraine said, reading the name. "Who is Jaime?"

"This kid was cleaning a display case. He must be an intern or something, but he told me he might know where we could get one of Pilar's paintings."

"It will be a fake," Lorraine said. "He probably has you marked as a dumb tourist in search of a bargain."

"Or something else," Connor said. "I can't believe I took a phone number from some limp-wristed kid who told me he gets off work in one hour."

"Well, I didn't get anywhere with Nils Van der Holt," Lorraine said. "So, it might be worth waiting an hour to call your little buddy Jaime just so this trip isn't a total waste of time."

"He isn't my little buddy."

"Easy, flyboy." Lorraine laughed. "Be nice to Jaime and maybe he'll tell us something useful. We can go down to the marina district and look at boats in the meantime."

"Right," Connor muttered. "You know me all too well, Peaches."

The Darkroom

"You owe me some gas money."

That was how Bennett greeted his brother in front of the train station in Providence that afternoon.

"Hit Dad up for a few bucks," Nathan said as he tossed his rucksack into the backseat of Bennett's jeep with Natalie.

"Mom and Dad are still in Florida," Bennett said, pointing to his gas needle, which was bouncing on empty. "And we're not going to get home on fumes."

"Great," Nathan said. "I'm home on winter break and they're not even here."

"That's okay," Natalie said. "Bertram is sitting in the living room waiting to see you."

"Of course," Nathan said, clearly not enthused.

Nathan handed his credit card to Bennett at the gas station—he filled up the Jeep while Nathan protested, "Just five dollars!"—and then they drove down the West Bay and across the bridges into Newport.

"Nathan," Bertram said, while Fenway circled and whined at the door when the young people came into the house. "It's good to see you, son. How are things at school?"

"Fine," Nathan said. "The drama club is doing a production of Thornton Wilder's *Our Town*."

"I'm more interested in your studies, Nathan."

"Oh, they're fine, too. Let me go upstairs and toss my bag in my room. I'll be right back."

When Nathan came back downstairs after washing his face and combing his hair, he first went to the kitchen to complain to Bennett.

"What did you guys do to my room?" Nathan said.

"That was Mom," Bennett said, as he foraged in the refrigerator for the ingredients for dinner. "Looks like we're having meatloaf tonight."

"Whatever," Nathan said. "What is all that crap she put up on my walls?"

"That's her research," Natalie said. "She's writing a book about the artist Pilar Vasquez."

"Really? She needs all those maps and pictures and stuff?"

"Yup," Bennett said. "You know how our mother likes to get the details straight."

"Well, I'm taking it all down while I'm home."

"Don't you dare," Bennett said, putting the meatloaf in the oven and setting the timer. "We helped her get everything arranged just right. You can hang out in my room."

"No way. I'm going to get a headache if I have to look at those pictures of the mountains and the moon the way she has them put up."

"Those pictures are important clues," Natalie said. "Your mother went to a lot of trouble to get pictures of Pilar's *Moons of The Sierra Maestra* out of books and catalogs and we've been trying to figure out the secret messages."

"If you had to tape them up all around my room, couldn't you at least put them in the right order?"

"They are in the right order," Bennett said. "All the ones with the cat in the foreground are together and so are the ones with the gate, the well, and also the stone ruins."

"You go up there and take a look," Nathan said, pointing upstairs. "You tell me if that's the way the moon waxes and wanes."

"Huh?"

"Don't you know that the new moon gets bright from right to left?" Nathan said. "The shadow gets smaller and smaller on the left side. That's called waxing. After the full moon the lighted portion is on the left and getting smaller every night, which is called waning."

"So?"

"If there's a message in those paintings, at least arrange them in a way that makes sense," Nathan said. "When you look around the room, you should be able to follow the phases of the moon in each picture the way it moves across the sky every month."

The three youngsters didn't realize that Bertram was standing in the doorway to the kitchen until he spoke.

"Bravo, Nathan," Bertram said. "I'm delighted that you've taken an interest in this mystery."

"I didn't say that, Grandfather. It's just that—"

"Nonsense," Bertram said, interrupting Nathan. "I know how your mind works. Once you engage a puzzle you must see it through to a solution."

"I guess so," Nathan said.

"Now there is another matter that you can assist us with. You remember how to develop 35mm film, I assume?"

"Yes," Nathan said. "But I haven't done any darkroom stuff in a long time."

"I can help," Bennett said. "Mom showed me how to do all that."

"If it's black and white, we should be able to develop the negatives," Nathan said, looking at Bennett.

"That dices it," Bertram said. "Let us proceed to Lorraine's darkroom. I'd like to have some prints to show her and Connor when they get home."

The four of them went to the basement and entered the darkroom that Connor had built for Lorraine years earlier. The walls were painted flat green, with a long kitchen-like counter on each side. The developing table had a sink and cabinets of chemicals, and the printing side was dominated by a Bessler MX45 enlarger, which could handle even the large-format film Lorraine occasionally used.

Fenway knew that Lorraine's darkroom was the one place in the house that was off limits to her so she settled on the floor outside the door to wait for Bennett to emerge.

"Good news," Nathan said, looking at the thermometer on the wall. "The temperature in here is sixty-eight, perfect for developing."

"Mom still keeps it that way," Bennett said as he put on a pair of surgical gloves.

"Okay," Nathan said. "Can you fill the beakers with the chemicals?"

"No problem," Bennett said. Then he filled beakers marked *develop*, *stop*, and *fix* with measured amounts of chemicals.

"This is exciting," Natalie said, when Nathan switched off the white lights. Then the room was illuminated by the shadowy glow of red lamps. "I love watching you two work together."

"Except that the last time we did this together," Nathan said as he extracted the film and wound it into an inversion canister, "Benny had to stand on a milk crate to reach the chemicals."

"I guess it has been a while," Bennett said.

"You can pour in the developer," Nathan said, holding the canister. "Remember, no bubbles."

"Got it," Bennett said.

Nathan set the timer and inverted the canister to mix the developing solution around the negatives. When it was time, he drained the developing solution and Bennett added the stop solution. Finally, they repeated the process once more with the fixing solution.

"Let me rinse it," Bennett said, and Nathan handed him the canister to be filled and drained with water. Then they took the strip of negatives out of the canister and hung it up to dry.

They went upstairs to the kitchen where Natalie steamed some vegetables before Bennett pulled the meatloaf from the oven. Bertram and Nathan sat down at the breakfast nook and allowed Bennett and Natalie to serve them dinner, topped off with an apple pie. After which Nathan said, "Not too shabby."

"You're welcome," Bennett said.

"Quite a fine meal," Bertram said. "Shall we go print our negatives?"

"You still haven't told me what these pictures are of," Nathan said as they trooped downstairs.

"You'll see," Bennett said.

Under the red lights once again, Nathan and Bennett prepared the trays of processing fluid and placed an eight by ten sheet of print paper under the enlarger.

"What the hell?" Bennett said when the image became clear. "This isn't it!"

"Watch your language," Bertram said.

"But this isn't the right picture," Bennett said.

"I can see that," Bertram said. "Perhaps the professor made a mistake. Let's print all the photographs on the roll."

"There are only three," Nathan said. "And they are all just like this—pictures of the Gettysburg Address."

"What does this mean?" Nathan asked after he turned the white lights on.

"It means that I've been an old fool," Bertram said.

Combat Cuisine

"I'm Connor Laird and this is my wife, Lorraine. Now what's this about a Pilar Vasquez painting?"

That was how Connor greeted Jaime when they met him at a café near the art gallery, where he was sitting alone at a table with his back to the wall. It was an artsy little place called Combat Cuisine, with walls painted in jungle camouflage colors and posters of Che Guevara and Patty Hearst over the kitchen. The side walls were lined with paintings tagged for sale, and when Jaime stood up to shake hands with Connor and Lorraine, they faced a slight young man with a sweet disposition.

"Thanks for meeting with us," Lorraine said. "I hope this won't cause you problems with Nils Van der Holt."

"We should be quick," Jaime said. "I'm an intern with Nils so if he saw me stealing his customers he might give the university a bad report. But please sit down."

"You've already been more helpful than Nils," Lorraine said. "He wouldn't even talk to us about Pilar's art."

"That's because he doesn't know anything about it," Jaime said. "Art is a commodity to men like him. All he sees is profit."

"So how do you know more than your boss?" Connor said.

"I'm an art history major with a thesis on Pilar Vasquez. I've always been fascinated by her legend."

"I take it your parents are from Cuba?"

"My grandparents," Jaime said. "So, if you don't mind me asking, why are you interested in paintings by an artist of the revolution?"

Lorraine said, "We're trying to find out what actually happened to Pilar."

"She's buried in Havana," Jaime said, "according to the art history textbooks."

"We don't believe that," Lorraine said. "And neither do you."

"You're right," the young man said. "But why do you care?"

Lorraine glanced at Connor before she said, "We're friends of her daughter."

"Which one?" Jaime said, with a laugh. "There have been a few imposters. Some people think there's a lot of money in Swiss banks."

"Our friend is no fake," Connor said. "She's the real deal."

"Is that why you carry a gun?"

"Sorry you noticed," Connor said, pulling the hem of his shirt down.

"It was hard not to see it when I was kneeling next to you in the gallery."

"Right. Let's just say that Pilar is tangled up with some rough characters and I like to be prepared."

"I see," Jaime said. "If I help you, maybe you could help me?"

"Here it is," Lorraine said. "We know that Pilar Vasquez was handled by some CIA types who meddled in Cuban affairs, and now we know that they also consorted with drug smugglers. I'm writing a book about it. That's all we can tell you right now."

When the waiter came over to take their order—a young man with tattoos, piercings, and spiked hair—Jaime motioned for him to sit alongside him.

"Ricky," Jaime said, "meet Lorraine and her bodyguard,"

"I'm her husband."

"Sorry," Jaime said. "Bodyguard sounds more exciting."

"Right." Connor said. "Then I'm her husband and her bodyguard. So, who are you, Ricky?"

"I'm an artist," Ricky said. "But I wait tables to pay the rent. I also get a commission on the paintings I sell."

"Are any of these your work?" Lorraine said.

"No," Ricky said, laughing. "You can't get my paintings inside. I tag."

"You do graffiti?" Connor said. "And that's what you call art?"

"People stop to look when Ricky tags a building," Jaime said. "Some people ask him to make something nice on their walls. You'd be amazed what he can do with a palette of rattle cans."

"I do nice work," Ricky said.

"I'm sure," Lorraine said. "Maybe you can point some of your work out to us sometime. But right now, we're looking for paintings by Pilar Vasquez."

"Okay," Jaime said, pointing over his shoulder. "What do you make of this?"

The small square painting on the wall between where the boys sat had a radiant gold cross in the upper left corner beaming down on a child leading a burro along a dirt path, with mountains and stars in the background.

"Oh my God," Lorraine said. "That could be by Pilar!"

"I don't see it," Connor said. "That's a religious painting and I can't imagine that the revolutionary artist who helped Fidel expel the church from Cuba would create such a thing."

"Look at the mountains in the background," Lorraine said.

"Right," Connor said. "That's the Sierra Maestra, exactly like Pilar painted it. Other than the religious angle, that is."

"You have a good eye," Jaime said. "Notice the raw style, the way the artist laid the paint on the canvas in alternating upstrokes and downstrokes, with occasional diagonal strokes. That says Pilar Vasquez to me."

"It's not signed by the artist," Ricky said. "So I can't claim it as Pilar Vasquez. But it could be by her."

"There's nothing on the back of the canvas?"

"Nothing," Ricky said.

"If I were you," Jaime said, "I would buy this painting right now. I'd do it myself if three hundred and fifty dollars wasn't impossible for me at the moment."

"Perhaps we will," Lorraine said. "Where did that painting come from?"

"I don't know," Ricky said. "Some guy brought it in and said it belonged to his aunt who passed away. I didn't think much of it until Jaime noticed it."

"My jaw dropped when I saw it," Jaime said. "This painting is only a few years old at the most. I'm mystified by it."

Lorraine said, "Do you have the contact information for the seller?"

"It was a very casual deal," Ricky said. "I don't even have a phone number. The guy comes by every few days and just looks in the window to see if it has sold yet. But when he comes in to collect his cash, I might be able to learn more."

"We need to know where his aunt got it," Connor said.

"That's what I want to know, too," Jaime said.

Lorraine turned to Connor and said, "What do you think?"

"I think Ali Vasquez is buying a painting," Connor said, reaching for the envelope of cash she had entrusted to him.

Connor peeled the cash and handed it to Ricky while Lorraine exchanged e-mail addresses and phone numbers with both boys. Then Jaime took the painting down and handed it to Lorraine.

"I hope to see this painting again someday," Jaime said.

"Don't worry, you'll be seeing us again," Connor said. "One way or the other."

CHAPTER

3

Friday, March 18, 2005

A Family Matter

"I'm afraid that Bennett and I have created a serious problem." Bertram said this to Lorraine and Connor over their morning coffee. They had arrived home on a flight from West Palm Beach well after midnight and had gone to bed without awakening him.

"What did Ben do now?" Lorraine said.

"Actually, Bennett simply made a youthful mistake," Bertram said, warming his hands over the woodstove. "It was I who turned it into a serious problem for the family."

"Oh boy," Connor said. "What now?"

"It seems that Ali's picture of Ernesto was not lost on the night we were attacked, as we had thought," Bertram said. "Bennett took it from the floor after Ransom dispatched Nikoli Volkov and secretly kept it all this time."

"Please tell me you're kidding," Connor said.

"Not in the slightest. Bennett picked up the picture and put it in his underwear. The FBI somehow missed it when they searched us."

"How could they miss that?" Lorraine said.

"Easy," Connor said. "They were looking for weapons at the scene of a home invasion and murder. There was no reason to further traumatize a teenage victim by sticking their fingers into his junk."

"So, what do we do now?" Lorraine asked. "Do we turn the picture and the microdot over to the FBI? Rene Garcia might go easy on Bennett that way."

"Hell no," Connor said. "Let's keep Ben out of this. Besides, Ali Vasquez needs that picture. The microdot might tell the full story of how the Russians destroyed her family."

"Unfortunately," Bertram said, "it's not going to be that easy. It seems that yesterday, after I discovered that Bennett had the picture, I committed a grievous misjudgment of my own."

"Dad," Lorraine said, "what did you do?"

"It so happens that I recognized the dot as an advanced type that could not be read under a typical laboratory microscope. So, we took it to the one person who I knew might have the requisite equipment—Professor Sergei Mikhailov at the Naval War College."

"A Russian?" Connor said. "You delivered Ali's microdot to the Russians?"

"Not quite," Bertram said. "Mikhailov is a former KGB man who has been thoroughly vetted to lecture on human intelligence techniques at the War College. He now helps us defend against the same techniques he once employed as a Soviet spy."

"He's still a damn Russian," Connor said.

"He is now an American citizen who has given us priceless insight into the Russian worldview, which we must understand if there is any hope of peacefully coexisting with them."

"I get that the Cold War is over," Lorraine said. "But where is Ali's picture now?" "I have the picture," Bertram said. "But Sergei Mikhailov removed the microdot to place it in a microscopic reading device. Then he used some sleight-of-hand to give us a meaningless dot, while keeping Ali's microdot for himself."

Connor rubbed his forehead and said, "Did you at least get to see what was on Ali's dot before he stole it?"

"Yes, it was a coded message using a Soviet cypher from the '60s. We thought we had a photograph of the message, but Sergei fooled us there, too. So, we have nothing."

"What options do we have now?" Lorraine said.

"We have to call Rene Garcia," Connor said. "No matter how bad it looks for us, we have to report that there is some sort of double agent at the War College. We can say that I had the picture, not Ben."

"Not so fast, Connor," Bertram said. "Saying anything but the absolute truth to the FBI is an invitation to disaster. Besides, I want a chance to talk to Sergei first."

"Fine," Connor said. "I'll go with you this time."

"I'm going to call our attorney," Lorraine said. "We have to make certain that Bennett is protected. The sooner we get Bill Gallo working on this the better."

"That's a good idea," Connor said. "But don't call Bill. Go to his office and speak face-to-face."

"Oh?" Lorraine said. "Do you think our phone calls are still being monitored?"

"Probably not," Bertram said. "But the FBI did have surveillance on you when Connor and Ali were suspects in the bombing. So better safe than sorry."

"What's the matter?" Connor said, after Lorraine took a deep breath to compose herself.

"It makes me sick to think that my own government might still be watching me—on my phone, on my computer, even in my home. We've got to get clear of this mess."

Saville Row

Ali traveled light, with just a carry-on bag, and arrived at Heathrow a little before 7 a.m. London time. She had booked a room at the Kensington Garden Hotel, where she freshened up before taking the underground to Oxford Circus. She felt energized when she walked into the design studios of Sophia Fuentes Lavallee on Saville Row.

Sophia's reception area was a tiny corner of the studio where a secretary sat. A man in a gray suit was reading a magazine, and a woman who had to be Sophia was visible at the far side of the work area, looking out the window with her arms folded across her chest.

"I'd like to have a word with Sophia. My name is Alicia Vasquez."

"Miss Lavallee does not accept walk-in clients. If you give me your information, perhaps I can have one of her associate designers contact you next week."

"This is more of a family matter," Ali said.

No sooner were the words out of Ali's mouth before she realized that the man with the magazine had stood up behind her. At the same time the designer turned from her perch at the window and studied Ali coolly.

"I'll see this one, Jerome," Sophia said after she had looked Ali over from head to toe.

Sophia steered Ali past the workers piecing together her creations to an office at the far side of the studio. There were couches and chairs to one side, but the designer took her battle station behind a modern chrome-and-glass executive desk and said, "What are you doing here?"

There was no chair in front of the desk for Ali, so the women stood and faced off across the barren plateau of glass. Sophia was older than Ali had expected, with features molded by years of unabashed surgery, Botox, and a robust spa regimen. Yet her hands, which were planted on the desktop with fingers spread, spoke of a woman well into middle age.

"You haven't given me a chance to introduce myself."

"I know who you are. I've had to suffer through the ridiculous accusations of that reporter Lorraine what's-her-name ever since *The Atlantic* magazine published her article."

"Then you know that I am Alicia—Pilar Vasquez's daughter."

"So you say. But even assuming that is true, what is it to me?"

"Pilar lived with Ernesto in the Sierra Maestra for several months before they left Cuba. That much is certain. I thought that—"

"You thought what? That you are entitled to money from Ernesto's estate? Get in line."

"No, I don't want money. I just want to know about my family."

"Your family?"

"Sophia, I can't know exactly what Pilar's relationship with Ernesto might have been, but I am almost certain that he was my father."

"That is scandalous trash!" Sophia said. "Pilar was my father's first cousin. They grew up in adjoining homes in the finest neighborhood of Havana."

"Sophia, my adopted father had a picture of Ernesto in his old photo album dating from before the Revolution."

"So? My father migrated from that godforsaken island after Castro came to power and started a new life on the pampas of Argentina. I remember the day he left us to pursue some crazy notion of liberating Cuba from a tyrant's grasp. Now you come here scratching around for money?"

"I'm not talking about money, Sophia. This is about family. We could be half-sisters."

"Ha! That is not possible. Look at you, in your bargain-basement rags with your street rabble demeanor—how could we be related?"

"I understand how upsetting this can be," Ali said. "But I've seen the evidence with my own eyes—including the wreckage of Ernesto's airplane in the Everglades."

"Let me tell you something before I have Jerome remove you," Sophia said. "Your pitiful attempt at extortion will soon be exposed. I have hired investigators who will prove that you are in no way related to Pilar Vasquez, much less Ernesto. You are a charlatan with green contact lenses to imitate Pilar's famous eyes who has concocted an elaborate scheme to connect Pilar to my father."

"Sophia, please listen. There is ample proof that they lived together in the Sierra Maestra after Pilar was released from prison."

"Enough of your nonsense! Pilar died in the *Presidio Modelo* and was buried in the *Cemetario de Christofo Colon* in Havana. Ernesto never again saw that harlot after she seduced him when he was only a child, which caused him to be sent to the wilderness of the Sierra Maestra."

"Sophia, I know about the money in Israel. I don't want any of that. I just want to know what happened to my family."

"You little tramp! The Vasquez family were plantation owners. Your inheritance is filthy riches, stripped from the backs of slaves. Do you understand that? The House of Vasquez owned human beings and forced them to labor in their sugarcane fields and coffee plantations until they died. They consumed lives. I wouldn't lower myself to touching that filthy money."

"Sophia, can't we just sit down and talk like sisters?"

"How dare you!" Sophia leaned across the glass plateau of her desk. "You cheap, no-class tramp. If Ernesto was careless with his seed, that would no more make us sisters than if he consorted with a prostitute. Get out of my studio!"

Ali turned and faced Jerome when she felt his hand firmly grasp her elbow. He steered her out of the studio without a word until she was out the door. When she was outside looking into the studio, Ali saw that none of the workers had looked up from their tasks as she was removed.

"I wouldn't return, miss," Jerome said. "It might be most unpleasant. Cheers."

Ali was stunned by Sophia's words. It had never occurred to her that the Vasquez family—her family—had owned slaves in Cuba. The thought baked into her brain while she looked up and down Saville Row to regain her bearings, realizing for the first time how out of place she must look to the hip Londoners walking by.

That was when Bernardo called her cell phone and said, "Can you meet me in Stuttgart this Monday?"

"I suppose," Ali said. "But why Stuttgart?"

"Because Stuttgart is where the great cars are."

Providence

Sergei Mikhailov was not answering his office telephone, so Connor and Bertram drove over to the Naval War College where they found a note on his door indicating that he would not be in to work that morning. But his home telephone and address were listed in the White Pages, so they drove up the East Bay to Providence and arrived in front of a tidy Dutch Colonial house on Rochambeau Avenue shortly after noon. The curtains in the Mikhailov home were drawn closed, so Connor used his cell phone to call Sergei's home telephone before they got out of his truck.

The call went to voicemail.

"Let's go ring the doorbell," Bertram said.

"Right," Connor said as he stepped out of the truck. "But if he doesn't come to the door, our next call has to be to Rene Garcia."

"Agreed," Bertram said as he bent down to pick up the plastic bag containing the day's copy of *The Providence Journal*, which had been dutifully deposited on the doorstep.

Connor reached for the doorbell, but the door cracked open before his arm was fully outstretched.

"Hello, Ambassador," Sergei Mikhailov said when the door was fully open. "Won't you please come in?"

"Thank you," Bertram said, handing Sergei his newspaper. "This is my son, Connor. I am confident that you know the purpose of this visit?"

The professor was a mess compared to how he had appeared in his office the previous day. Stooped over and unkempt, he appeared to be dressed in the same day-old clothes. His hands were trembling—he appeared to be sweating—and his eyes, which had been probing and steady, had become shifty and unsure.

"Oh?" Sergei said. "Your son, the airline pilot? I had expected the FBI to be at my door this morning."

"Let's hope that won't be necessary," Bertram said. "Do you have my item?"

"Yes." Sergei reached into his pocket. "Yes of course, Ambassador. Here it is."

"This better not be another stunt," Connor said, when Bertram handed the small container with the microdot to him for safekeeping.

"I assure you that that is the item you brought to my office yesterday. I beg your forgiveness, Ambassador Calhoun. Won't you sit down and allow me to explain?"

"Of course."

Sergei's wife appeared with a tray of tea as soon as they had taken their seats and promptly disappeared back into the kitchen without a word.

"I don't know what came over me yesterday," Sergei said, as he poured them each a cup of tea. "I suppose old habits die hard. But when I saw that item I immediately realized that it must be extraordinarily valuable. My hands performed the theft before my mind realized what I had done."

"I understand," Bertram said, taking a teacup out of Sergei's hand.

"Bertram," Connor said, pausing over the tea. "Are you sure this is okay?"

"What is your concern, Connor?"

"You know how the KGB likes to get rid of troublemakers."

"Please," Sergei said, taking a sip of the tea. "Stronium-210 is a most difficult isotope to handle. An old fool like me wouldn't dare touch it."

"Right," Connor said, putting down the teacup. "I'm not a big fan of tea anyway."

"Perhaps we are both old fools," Bertram said. "That is exactly how I felt when my grandsons developed your film last night."

"Of course," Sergei said, and shook his head. "If I had been thinking clearly, I would have known that an accomplished photographer such as your daughter would have a darkroom in her home. As it was I expected that it might take you longer to view the pictures I had taken."

"Tell me one thing," Connor said. "How much money did you think you would get if you sold this item?"

"Perhaps as much as one million dollars," Sergei said. "That did not seem like an unreasonable amount, in that Nikoli Volkov had recently been expelled from the Russian Federation's delegation to the United Nations."

"Volkov?" Connor said. "How did you connect this item to him?"

"A young man named Bennett mentioned his name."

"Right," Connor said, shooting an icy stare at Bertram when his son's name was used. "We got what we came for, Bertram. Let's hit the road."

"Yes." Bertram stood up slowly. "We'll have to continue this discussion at a later date. Until then, I suggest that you carry on with your normal routine, Sergei."

"Are you implying that you are not going to report this misadventure to the authorities, Ambassador?"

"For now, that doesn't seem necessary. Good day, old friend."

Bertram and Connor stepped outside into a sunny day. With no wind, they hardly felt the cold.

"Dammit, Dad," Connor said, walking to his truck. "Why in the world did you drag Ben even deeper into this mess? Now it's not just interfering with an investigation and tampering with evidence—now he might be a teenager convicted of espionage."

"It was a teaching moment, Connor. Unfortunately, it did not have the desired effect."

"To say the least. And why would you pretend this never happened with Sergei? He can't possibly go back to the War College now that we know he still has KGB tendencies."

Before Bertram could utter an answer, two dark blue SUVs came down Rochambeau Avenue from opposite directions and stopped next to where Connor's truck was parked.

"Screw me," Connor said, when Special Agent Rene Garcia dismounted from the lead SUV and walked directly toward them.

Wickford Bellingham

Lorraine was at City Hall on a story for the newspaper when Bertram called and instructed her to come to Providence with Bennett forthwith. Her son had just come home from school with Natalie when she called him.

"Put on chinos and a tie, Bennett. We're going to see Rene Garcia at the Federal Building in Providence."

"How come?"

"I'll explain later. Your grandfather wants you to bring the snapshot of Ernesto. He said that it's in the Bible next to his bed."

"Uh-oh. That doesn't sound good. Is Natalie coming?"

"Absolutely not. Natalie should go home and stay there." Lorraine remembered that their calls might be monitored when she added, "Natalie Lopes has nothing to do with this. Nothing at all."

However, Natalie was still at the Laird home when Lorraine pulled into the driveway a few minutes later. She and Nathan were poring over the prints of the *Moons of the Sierra Maestra* on the dining room table.

"Natalie, you should go home until this mess blows over."

"I can't," she said. "I'm helping Nathan. He's on to something here."

"We're counting the stars," Nathan said. "See? There are different numbers of stars east and west of the moon in each picture. And we're giving a higher value to the big stars—say ten, for now. The numbers we come up with must mean something."

"I see that," Lorraine said. "The trick is to make sense of the numbers. Any ideas?"

"They could be coordinates," Natalie said. "My father uses radio navigation lines that are numbers on the nautical chart to find his lobster traps in the fog."

"Or latitudes and longitudes," Nathan said. "Maybe Dad can take a look at these numbers when he gets home."

"Okay," Lorraine said. "Bertram and I were thinking along those same lines. These might be the numbers to secret bank accounts for all we know. We just have to come up with the right numbers. So, stick with it."

Lorraine and Bennett left for Providence as soon as he emerged from Bertram's room with the snapshot in hand. They took the less direct but faster route into the city on the interstate and soon they were standing in the reception room of the FBI office in the Senator John O. Pastore Federal Building. A female agent took Bennett directly to a conference room while Lorraine was invited into Special Agent Rene Garcia's office, where Bertram and Connor were waiting.

"Normally we only allow one of the parents to watch," Garcia said, when he turned off the lights in his office and opened the venetian blinds on the one-way glass. "But you might as well all hear this. We'll see how it goes."

"I'm glad Bill is in there," Lorraine said, when she saw that Attorney William Gallo was seated in the room alongside Bennett.

"Ben is not an idiot," Connor said. "He knows his whole future is on the line in there. He'll do the right thing."

"Why aren't you conducting the interview?" Lorraine said.

"Bennett already knows me," Garcia said. "I want him to tell his story to someone fair and impartial. Linda is the best interviewer in our office."

As it was, the interview lasted nearly two full hours, which was the most nonstop talking any of the family had ever heard from Bennett. He sat upright the entire time and answered each question clearly and truthfully in logically arranged sentences, looking directly at the agent.

When it was over, he had covered every detail of the events as he had personally experienced them, without straying into speculation.

"Damn," Connor said, when Bennett and the agent stood up and shook hands at the end. "That was perfect. I had no idea he could speak that well."

"You should read his poetry," Lorraine said. "Sometime I'll show you a few of the little notes he leaves for me find."

"That I have to see," Connor said.

They were reunited with Bennett in the waiting room, where Rene Garcia asked them to remain while he and Linda dissected Bennett's statement.

"I've never been prouder of you," Bertram said when he hugged Bennett.

"Can we go home now?" the teenager said, clearly embarrassed by the attention.

"Hang tight," Connor said. "Garcia wants to talk to us."

When Garcia emerged from the interview room a short time later, he asked all of them to follow him out of the office.

"Where are we going?" Bertram said.

"The US Attorney would like to speak with all of you," Garcia said as they boarded an elevator to go upstairs.

"Quite frankly," Garcia said, when the doors enclosed them in the elevator cab, "I believe that a number of crimes have been committed here."

Bill Gallo only nodded at that comment, but Bertram said, "That's unfortunate."

"What I believe doesn't matter," Garcia said. "I simply make the best case I can and present the facts to the US Attorney. We'll see what he says."

"Anyway, this building is really something," Bennett said, admiring the marble floors, oak doors, and brass fixtures outside the US Attorney's office.

"Right," Connor said. "They built this place back when the government was running with a surplus."

Wickford Bellingham was waiting behind an enormous oak desk in his corner office. The US Attorney for Rhode Island was a former mayor of the second largest city in the state, ex-president of the state senate, and one-time state attorney general. It was widely accepted that he would be the next governor.

"Ambassador Calhoun," the old pol said in the flourished baritone voice of a professional orator when he stood to shake hands. "This is an honor."

"Indeed," Bertram said, with a nod.

"Hello, Wick," Bill Gallo said.

"Hello, Bill. I should have guessed they would bring you along."

"It's always a pleasure."

"And, hello, Lorraine." Wick Bellingham turned to her. "You beat me up pretty good in that article you did on vending machines and organized crime in Newport."

"I strive for accuracy, sir. If you believe I misrepresented the facts, I'd like to hear about it."

"I knew you'd say that," he said with a laugh. "Anyway, we've got to be able to roll with the punches in this business. Won't you sit down?"

"So," Wick said. "Special Agent Garcia, where do we stand on this matter?"

"Conspiracy to interfere with a federal investigation, concealing evidence, tampering with evidence, and possibly espionage."

"What about lying to the FBI?" Wick said. "That's usually your slam-dunk."

"I don't see any reason to charge Bennett Laird with that," Garcia said. "He appears to have been forthright and helpful during his interview."

"Nonetheless, those are serious charges."

"That's only to date," Garcia said. "I have every reason to believe that this family is still interfering in the Vasquez investigation."

"That is certainly true for me," Lorraine said. "This could be a freedom-of-the-press issue."

"Please," Wick said, raising a hand to stop her. "The *Newport Daily News* isn't the *New York Times* or the *Washington Post* but a black eye from your pen really hurts in this little state."

"If I may say so," Garcia said, "I don't see intent here. These people seem to be motivated by a genuine desire to assist Alicia Vasquez. So I'm willing to forgive some subterfuge, under the circumstances."

"Well, Rene," Wick said, "thanks for dumping this one in my lap. Now I'm sitting here with one of the most respected men in government—no president or senator would refuse a phone call from Ambassador Bertram Calhoun—and I'm wondering what I should do about his family.

"You know," Wick continued, waving a hand at the group. "You people are like a one-household wrecking crew with exploding airplanes, gun battles in the Florida Keys, and now meetings with foreign operatives right here in my backyard. And you're not done apparently, unless I charge you with some crimes."

"Now this is getting interesting," Bill said.

"Take it easy, Bill. No charges are coming today."

"This story isn't going away," Lorraine said.

"Of course not. We all know that when you and Connor latch on to some cause there's no letting go. What troubles me is that now there seems to be another generation of muckrakers sticking their noses in where they don't belong. Young man, what were you thinking when you removed a vital piece of evidence from a crime scene?"

"I guess I wasn't thinking at all," Bennett said.

"Obviously not. Now I'm contemplating imposing some restrictions on your activities for your own good. Perhaps a travel ban for all of you."

"Captain Laird is an airline pilot," Bill said. "He has to travel."

"Ditto for a diplomat and a journalist," Lorraine said.

"I can see that you are all going to be thorns under my saddle," Wick Bellingham said. "And, Bill, don't sit there giving me that famous I-can't-wait-to-get-you-in-a-courtroom smile. It won't work on me."

"Maybe it already has," Bill said with a nod.

"You're right that I want to stay out of court with this, but not because of your cross-examination antics. After all, national security is involved here, and we'll have to see how this microdot nonsense plays with the intelligence community. Let me just be clear that this investigation is not closed by any means. I'm going to refer all of this to the US Attorney in Miami who is handling the Vasquez case. Maybe he can figure out what charges to bring against you, if any."

"That's a good way to stay out of a courtroom," Bill said.

"Whatever," Wick Bellingham said with a laugh. "Now get out of my office, Bill. And take these hooligans along with you."

They were all out of the office and going down on the elevator when Garcia said, "Don't forget, Connor, I have the keys to your truck in my office."

"Right." Connor turned to the group. "Bertram, why don't you go home with Lorraine and Bennett?"

"Thanks for going to bat for us in there," Connor said when he and Garcia were alone in the agent's office.

"Did I help you out?" Garcia said.

"Sure. You gave Wick Bellingham reasons to pass the buck to the US Attorney in Miami, who probably doesn't really care about our involvement in his case. I appreciate it."

"Maybe I did," Garcia said, barely showing his teeth in a wry smile. "Then again, maybe I just handed you a shovel to dig a deeper hole for yourself."

CHAPTER

4

Saturday, March 19, 2005

Republic of Estonia

There were no direct flights from London to Estonia, so Ali took Finnair to Helsinki and boarded a short connecting flight across the Baltic Sea to Tallinn, the capital and largest city of the former Soviet state. From there a two-and-a-half-hour train ride brought her to Narva, a modern city in the northeast corner of the country.

She had purchased an Estonian phrase book at the airport in Tallinn and converted some dollars to *kroons*, but when she showed Rose's address to the cab driver at the train station, he said, "Okay, five dollars American?"

It was late afternoon by the time Ali stepped out of the taxi in front of Rose's apartment building. When she pressed the buzzer on the intercom at the front door, she had not seen nor spoken to her adopted mother in over a month.

"Hello, Mother. May I come in?"

"Alicia?" Rose said after a few moments of stunned silence. "Is that you?"

"Yes, Rose. May I come up? I'd like to see you."

After what seemed like a lifetime of silence Rose said, "Come upstairs," and the door buzzed and unlocked for Ali to enter.

"I'm so sorry," Rose said when she hugged Ali at the door to her apartment. "I had to sell the house and leave so suddenly. It was awful! But here you are."

"I'm sorry too, Rose. I should have called, but I've been in the shadows."

"Never mind, I'm so happy you are here. But what if I wasn't home today?"

"There are many hotels in Narva," Ali said.

"Of course," Rose said, placing a teakettle on the stove. "How long can you stay with me?"

"Come Monday morning I have to be in Stuttgart."

"Oh?"

"I'm meeting a lawyer from Miami there. We're going to Credit Suisse in Zurich."

"Oh, oh, oh," Rose said. "That reminds me, I have to make one phone call. Please make yourself at home."

When Ali was alone, she looked around the apartment for something familiar but the only decoration she could see was a large bronze sun image in the tiny living room. Then she realized that Rose had not brought a single thing from her house in Maryland—not the furniture, appliances, or utensils—even Rose's clothes were different.

Going farther inside, Ali saw that the rear windows of the apartment overlooked some small buildings and beyond those rooftops, a narrow river. She could see the tower of an ancient castle and a bridge full of slow-moving trucks in the early blush of the long, beautiful Nordic twilight.

"What town is that across the river?" Ali asked.

"That's Russia, dear. Ivangorod, Russia."

Revelations

"How can you be certain that Sergei gave you the right microdot this time?"

Natalie asked this as she sat down between Bennett and Nathan for breakfast in the Lairds' kitchen while hard rain pelted the windows.

"That's right," Nathan said. "Maybe he pulled the old switcheroo on you again."

"I doubt that," Connor said. "The FBI has the dot now and they'll know for certain if it is a fake."

"Absolutely," Bertram said. "The NSA will be able to read the code, and if Sergei is not being forthright with the FBI, he might be spending the rest of his life in prison."

"What if he gave the bad guys pictures of the message on the microdot?" Natalie said. "Wouldn't that be just as good?"

"Not at all," Bertram said. "The Russians know perfectly well what the code on the microdot says because they wrote it and sent it to our rogue CIA friends years ago. They wanted the original dot back since it appears to be physical evidence of some very bad behavior on their account."

"That's right," Connor said. "Considering that they were willing to do away with all of us at Ransom's place, I'd say they were desperate to get that microdot back."

"Not all of us," Nathan said. "I missed out on that adventure."

"You didn't miss much," Bennett said. "We were lucky to get out of there alive."

"No," Connor said, "our luck was to have Vicente Molina on our side. He and Ransom saved our skins and don't you ever forget it."

"You and Mom were awesome, too," Bennett said.

"Darn it," Lorraine said when she heard her cell phone ringing in the kitchen. "There's my phone. Excuse me."

As she stood Bertram said, "Not at mealtime, Peaches. Let them leave a message."

"Ordinarily I'd agree," Lorraine said as she disappeared into the kitchen. "But this might be a very important call."

"You know, I've been thinking," Bennett said. "What if the numbers we're seeing in Pilar's paintings are the same code as what's on the microdot?"

"There's no way they'd add up," Nathan said. "The microdot had groups of five digits and the stars in the paintings add up to larger numbers."

"Maybe we're reading the paintings wrong," Natalie said. "What if the items in the foreground mean something? Like a cat is considered the guardian of the underworld and a gate symbolizes the Garden of Eden?"

"Where did you come up with that?" Bennett said.

"In a book about dream symbols," Natalie said.

"Ahem," Bertram said, clearing his throat. "You've all presented very thoughtful theories today, but I now know what the numbers of stars represent, and to whom they were addressed. Read me one group, Nathan."

"Here's one from a painting with a goat in the foreground," Nathan said, reading from a note card. "The big and small stars add up to nineteen on the left side of the moon and eighteen on the right."

"Ah yes," Bertram said, "this one is easy. The goat represents the scapegoat in Leviticus, so chapter 19, verse 18 would be, 'Do not seek revenge or bear a grudge against anyone among your people, but love your neighbor as yourself.'"

"I guess?" Nathan said. "How about this picture with a dove in the foreground. The stars add up to eighteen on the left and ten on the right."

"Very well," Bertram said, "if we take the dove as a symbol for the angel in Matthew that would be Matthew 18:10, 'Do not despise one of these little ones, for I tell you that their angels in heaven always see the face of my Father in heaven.'"

"No offense," Connor said, "but Pilar was tight with Fidel when he expelled the church from Cuba. So religious messages in her paintings don't make any sense to me at all."

"Of course, it wouldn't," Bertram said. "You're not a person of faith."

"I wouldn't say that. It takes lots of faith to take off in an airplane on a stormy night so my faith is reserved for things I can touch and facts I can use. My point is that in a book as large and rambling as the King James Bible, you can take almost any numbers and assign one of the verses to them."

"These meanings are clear despite your skepticism," Bertram said. "Remember that the *Moons of the Sierra Maestra* were painted after Pilar was released from prison and living with Ernesto. I am certain that she had found her faith and that the Moon paintings were meant as messages to her unborn child."

"You mean the Moons were meant for Ali?" Natalie said.

"That is exactly correct," Bertram said.

That was when Lorraine came back to the table.

"Connor," she said, "that call was from Jaime in West Palm Beach. The seller came to collect his money for the painting."

"Did he get the guy's address or phone number?"

"No," Lorraine said. "But he's pretty sure he knows where the man will be on Monday morning."

"Wait a minute," Bennett said. "Does that mean we're going to Florida to find where Pilar's new painting came from?"

"You're not going anywhere," Connor said. "You're grounded, hotshot."

"Yes," Lorraine said. "But we could use a good code-breaker on this trip. So, Nathan, how would you like to spend a few days of your spring break in Florida with Mom and Dad?"

"Gee," Nathan said, bowing his head. "Isn't that every college kid's dream?"

Across the Narva

"Rose, how much did you know?"

Ali asked this while they were still at the table after a light meal in her adopted mother's kitchen. One side of the table was against the window overlooking the Narva River.

"I didn't ask questions," Rose said, getting up to clear the dishes. "I was filled with joy when Arthur brought you home to be our daughter. Nothing else mattered."

"Rose, you are my mother—the only mother I have ever known. Pilar is a stranger to me and always will be. But I have to know where I came from, and only you can tell me that."

The older woman sat across from Ali and reached for her hands on the table.

"I remember the day Arthur brought you home. You were so small! He handed you to me and said, 'This is your daughter, Alicia.'"

"There's so much more, Rose. Please tell me."

"It's awful, dear. I don't like to think about it."

"You've always told me that my birth parents were killed in an airplane accident," Ali said. "I've often thought that was why I became a pilot, to be closer to them. But now I know that their crash was no accident, Rose."

"The government," Rose said, her voice trailing to a whisper. "Arthur only did what the government demanded."

"No, Rose. I know the truth now, that the man we knew as Arthur Johnson was really Johan Armbrust and that he was no longer with the National Security Agency. I know that the scientific equipment in his study was used to create microdots for communicating with the Cuban and Russian governments. And I know that he and Karl Olson staged the airplane crash in the Everglades to get rid of Pilar and Ernesto."

"He was a good man," Rose said.

"What did you know, Rose? Why did you tell me that my name had been Vasquez and that I should stay out of sight lest the Cuba men come and take me away to that terrible island?"

"I was always protecting you, Alicia. Arthur and I both wanted the best for you."

"Rose, we both know that Arthur did not take his own life that day. Karl Olson came into your home and murdered him. You do know that, don't you?"

"Yes—and I had to leave, to come here."

"You know everything, Rose, and soon I will too. But there is only one thing I'll ask you to tell me. If you love me, Rose—tell me why I am still alive."

"They let us keep you because we loved you, Alicia."

"There is more than that. Why did they wait thirty-two years to kill Arthur and try to get to me?"

"I—don't—know."

"They waited three decades to try to kidnap me again and they sent an agent to kill me in Florida, but some very brave men saved me. Then they attempted to murder a planeload of innocent people to get to me and Connor. You must know why they wish me to be dead after so many years, Rose. You must tell me, please."

"I'm so tired," Rose said, rising with difficulty. "I must lie down, Alicia dearest."

When Rose closed the door to her bedroom, Ali exhaled and went to check that the doors to her apartment were dead-bolted. She felt light-headed and vaguely uneasy when she came back to the kitchen with her notebook computer and opened it on the table.

I'll sleep on the sofa, Ali thought, *and leave at dawn. Rose has done enough.*

She was not surprised when she easily signed in on the internet since it was well known that Estonia was one of the most connected and tech-savvy countries on Earth. But when she sent an email to Lorraine, Ali was astonished that she replied almost instantly.

Of course, she thought. *Estonia is seven hours ahead of Rhode Island so it would be noontime there.*

Ali,

When are you coming home? A college boy named Jaime in West Palm Beach helped Connor and I locate a recent painting that is almost certainly by Pilar! The paint is very new on this canvas and when the seller collects his money we may be able to trace it back to the place of origin. We'll meet you in Miami. Be careful!

—Lorraine

Ali was stunned and still trying to digest the significance of Lorraine's message when she responded that she was meeting Bernardo in Stuttgart on Monday and then going to Zurich, and that she would hurry back to Miami soon after that. Then she just stared at the computer screen, slowly grasping the import of Lorraine's words—Pilar was alive!

When she re-read the message, Ali became aware that she was having trouble focusing on the screen. Her eyes ached, but why shouldn't they? She had come nearly halfway around the world with little sleep to meet her bitch of a half-sister and the adopted mother whom she now felt uncomfortably disconnected from.

She found herself rubbing her brow, just above her eyes, when her stomach became upset.

There was ringing—no, buzzing—in her ears.

Something I ate? Ali thought.

She looked out the window to the lights across the dark river, her vision blurry, and knew she had to get to the bathroom, stumbling on the way.

When she leaned over the toilet, Ali found that she could not vomit. She was breathing hard when she laid her head on the cold tile floor, thinking though a fog, *what is happening to me?*

She was not sure how long she was down or if she had been unconscious or not when she stood again and stumbled into the living room at the front of Rose's apartment. She felt better on the sofa and rolled to her side, pushing her face into the cushion.

When the buzzing began again, like an angry insect in her brain, she looked at the door to the apartment and stifled the urge to run outside into the night.

No, Ali thought, *I'm not crazy, there is something in these walls!*

She stood and searched around the living room, looking behind the furniture and touching the wallpaper, feeling faint and queasy. Until she touched the copper sun decoration and felt a tingling in her fingers.

What? she thought. *What is this thing?*

She tried to pry the decoration off the wall before she discovered that it could be easily lifted straight up off two mounting hooks.

Maybe I am crazy, she thought, when she held the decoration in her hands. *There's nothing to this thing.*

It was unremarkable and light to hold, obviously stamped out of one piece of copper with rays emanating like spokes from a polished half-dome about the size of a dinner plate. But although she still felt queasy, the buzzing and vibrating in her head had stopped.

When Ali turned around, she saw that the hollow decoration had been affixed to the wall in line with the window in the kitchen—looking directly across the Narva River to the lights in Russia.

No, Ali thought, *it can't be …*

CHAPTER

5

Monday, March 21, 2005

The Global Laundromat

Bernardo was waiting for Ali at the airport in Stuttgart on Monday morning, driving a low-slung and powerful Mercedes-Benz.

"Where did you get this car?" Ali said after she tossed her carry-on bag into the back.

"As an amateur race driver I have a relationship with the company," Bernardo said, pulling away from the curb. "So, whenever I'm on the Continent I fly directly to Stuttgart and pick up a special loaner. Be sure to fasten your seatbelt."

"Where are we going?"

"Zurich is about two hours on A81, although I can probably shave half an hour off that."

The car's engine was purring effortlessly on the autobahn when he glanced at her and said, "Are you feeling okay, Ali?"

"Actually, no. The doctor in Helsinki saw fluid in my ear and said I had the flu, but don't worry, I'm not contagious. I think it was food poisoning or something."

"Helsinki? I take it that your meeting with Sophia did not go well if you didn't stay in London the whole weekend."

"Unfortunately, that sisterly reunion was more of a confrontation,"

Ali said. "Anyway, I went to Estonia the next day to see my adopted mother for the first time in several months. That's where I got sick."

"But why Helsinki?"

"I couldn't stay with Rose. Something there was making me ill, so I left early Sunday morning and flew to Finland and checked into a hotel. I knew I could get plenty of rest and do some laundry there."

"You do travel light," Bernardo said. "I find that to be a refreshing change from some women I've traveled with."

"Oh?" Ali said. "Who are your usual traveling companions, Bernardo?"

"Just friends," he said, and smiled at her.

"One hundred and sixty kilometers per hour," Ali said, glancing at the speedometer. "Isn't that about one hundred miles per hour?"

"Yes," he said, relaxed and confident behind the wheel. "This is my therapy. Swiss lawyers sometimes talk endlessly, so knowing that a fine automobile is waiting outside makes these meetings bearable."

"That's nice," Ali said. "If you don't mind, I might just recline this seat and take a nap."

"Be my guest."

After less than two hours on the autobahn they entered Zurich and found Herr Rochat's office in a narrow brick building on Loewen Strasse, in the old city.

Herbert Rochat greeted them enthusiastically. He was a short, plump man with crystal-clear bifocals and soft hands, which Ali noticed were perfectly manicured. He had often worked with Vicente Molina in cases involving Cuban expatriates, but he had never met Bernardo.

"I greatly admired your father," he said. "He was the most courageous attorney I have ever met."

Herr Rochat then launched into a dissertation on the history of Swiss banking laws, emphasizing that—contrary to popular belief—these institutions were no haven for criminals and corrupt politicians and that every effort was made to return funds obtained by unscrupulous means to the rightful owners.

"That is why we are here," Bernardo said. "What can you tell us about the Vasquez family account?"

"Yes, of course," Herr Rochat said. "Miss Vasquez, I trust you have your passport? As you may know, the account in question was opened by the Vasquez family in 1947," Rochat said after he made a copy of Ali's passport and returned the document to her. "The major portion of this fortune transferred to you, Alicia Vasquez, in accordance with the Last Will and Testament of Pilar Vasquez, which was enrolled in the records of Collier County, Florida, in March of 1972."

"Let me guess," Ali said after exhaling. "All that was done by Judge Robert Lee Culpepper."

"Quite true," Rochat said. "And I must say, although I'm not formally trained in American law, it does seem somewhat unusual that a Federal Circuit Court handled your adoption and the transfer of that much wealth across national borders at the same time. However, the documents have withstood all legal reviews since then."

"I'm discovering that old Robert Lee Culpepper's power was absolute in 1972," Ali said. "How much money are we talking about?"

"Then, nearly ninety million US dollars."

"What about now?" Ali said.

"Now the balance is zero," Rochat said, somewhat surprised. "You—or someone representing themselves as you—closed the account five months ago on October 29, 2004."

"The hell I did," Ali said, turning to Bernardo. "I never even knew about this account."

"Take it easy, Ali," Bernardo said, with a hand on her forearm. "We'll figure this out, one step at a time."

Bernardo turned to Herr Rochat when he said, "My father's notes indicated that funds were being distributed from the Vasquez account for many years."

"That is correct," Herr Rochat said. "Two monthly allotments had been in effect since 1972. The funds for Alicia Vasquez—which were considerable—were directed to Tampa, Florida, where they were masked by a Federal witness protection program."

"Good old Robert Lee Culpepper again," Ali said.

"Yes," Herr Rochat said. "Although I would describe Judge Culpepper's legal construct as the most elegant money-laundering scheme I have ever personally witnessed, and I have seen a few. I was honored to work with Vicente in the matter of attempting to follow those protected transfers to you, Miss Vasquez. That was why Vicente was quite alarmed to see that the account was closed just when he was close to finally contacting you."

"I never saw any of that money," Ali said. "It must have gone to my adopted father and his partner in crime, Karl Olson."

"You said there were two monthly allotments," Bernardo said. "Where was the other allotment directed?"

"I'm afraid that I cannot discuss that matter," Rochat said. "Those funds were partitioned in a manner beyond disclosure in accordance with Pilar Vasquez's final wishes."

"Wait a minute," Ali said. "Did that other allotment go to Sofia Lavallee? Or is there another sibling I don't know about? Please tell me."

"I cannot do that," Herr Rochat said. "Again, Pilar—through Justice Culpepper—made it clear that the recipient of the second allotment should never be disclosed."

"Screw that," Ali said. "I have a right to know, don't I?"

Then she turned to Bernardo and said, "Do some of that lawyer stuff, Bernardo. Make a motion, or whatever. Get him to tell me who was getting that money."

"Easy, Ali," Bernardo said. "You don't mean that. Herr Rochat has been kind enough to bring us this far. You owe him a debt of gratitude."

"I suppose so," Ali said. "I'm sorry, Herr Rochat."

"That's quite all right," Rochat said. "No apology is necessary."

"The other allotment is of little import at this time," Bernardo said. "The big question is, where did the Vasquez fortune go when the account was closed?"

"Have you ever heard of the Global Laundromat?" Herr Rochat said. "Moldova?"

"Absolutely," Rochat said. "The Vasquez fortune went directly to Moldinconbank, where Russian investors used the funds to guarantee a loan to a fictitious company in London through their commercial bank, Traska Komercbanka in Riga, Latvia. Of course, the fake company with a London address could not return the investment, and Moldova judges quickly authenticated the debt and ordered the transfer of the funds to Traska Komercbanka. It was all done literally overnight."

"That's it?" Ali said. "Millions of dollars that Pilar left to me are gone and you can't even tell me where it went?"

"It isn't over," Bernardo said. "The transfer of funds to Moldova was obviously done illegally, since you clearly did not consent to the action."

"Sadly," Herr Rochat said, "you may find that the corruption of the Moldovan system is impenetrable. As an attorney, and as your father's son, you must be aware that the government of Russia is a large criminal enterprise dedicated to protecting a host of smaller criminal enterprises. However, if you authorize me to proceed, I may be able to make some discreet inquiries."

"Go for it," Ali said. "Just be careful, please. These people will stop at nothing to hide their dirty work."

"Perhaps we can continue this discussion tomorrow," Bernardo said. "Miss Vasquez has traveled great distances in the past few days and she may need some time to digest this information."

"Of course," the Swiss lawyer said. "Until tomorrow."

At the door, Herr Rochat asked Ali to stay behind momentarily while he said a few quiet words to her. Bernardo waited near the car while they spoke, out of earshot.

"How are you feeling?" Bernardo said, after she joined him on Loewen Strasse.

"My head is spinning. This is all happening so fast."

"Then let's check into our hotel," Bernardo said. "When you're ready we can have a bite to eat. We should enjoy ourselves while we are in this beautiful old city, don't you think?"

Speedball Summer

The offices of the *Newport Daily News* were located on Admiral Kalfbus Road, adjacent to the Navy base and the Naval War College. So, after the Monday morning editorial meeting Lorraine drove over to Coasters Harbor.

She had stopped her Volvo in the staff parking lot at the Naval War College to take a picture of Sergei Mikhailov's car in his assigned parking spot when a dark blue Jeep SUV pulled behind her.

"Good morning, Lorraine," Rene Garcia said, after he stepped up to her car. His leather coat was open, revealing the pistol and gold badge on his belt, and he had the scruffy look of a man who hadn't slept the previous night, rumpled and unshaven.

"I have no intention of contacting Professor Mikhailov," she said.

"Then why are you here?"

"I wanted to see if his car was in the parking lot, which it is, right there."

"And why is that of interest to you?"

"As a reporter, I have to ask why a known KGB man has an office in the building where all the navies of the free world talk strategy and international politics. Doesn't that seem odd?"

"A former KGB man," Garcia said. "And he has no access to classified information. All of that material is highly compartmentalized."

"Maybe not, but many of the naval officers he talks to every day are on the fast track to becoming admirals. So how do you know he doesn't report back to Mother Russia about the personalities and foibles of our people? You know that Russian State Security keeps dossiers on all of our key military and political leaders, looking for flaws to exploit."

Garcia studied her eyes for a few seconds before he said, "Let's go someplace and talk, Lorraine. If you stay here, I may have to arrest you for violating your no-contact order with Mikhailov."

"That's fine. How about the officers' club and marina?"

"I'll follow you."

Lorraine was in full reporter mode when she drove the short distance to the o-club on the narrow and well-groomed roads of the base, noting the time and dictating some details of the initial encounter with Garcia into her mini-recorder. Then she parked at the high end of the lot overlooking the marina with a commanding view of the choppy water of Narragansett Bay and the abutments of the Verrazano-Pell Bridge.

She thought about keeping the recorder turned on in her pocket in case Garcia was willing to talk outside, in the open. But it was a blustery day near the water and he asked her to sit in his SUV, so she turned the device off and tossed it on the seat of her Volvo.

"What brings you to Newport this morning, Special Agent Garcia? Have you been spying on my house again?"

"No, I was up all night, but not at your house. We got a tip on another case that didn't pan out. I was on my way home when I decided to swing through the Navy base."

"Oh?" Lorraine said. "That sounds like you were on a stakeout—in my city."

"I have several active investigations on my desk right now," Garcia said. "You know I can't tell you about any of them."

"I see," Lorraine said. "So, are you ready to talk about Sergei Mikhailov, off the record?"

"There's no such thing as off the record, Lorraine. All I ask is that you don't torpedo my investigation by revealing critical information, whether you hear it from me or someone else. Wait until after we get indictments and convictions. Isn't that what we both want?"

"That's fine. But if we put our cards on the table, you'll see that I have more questions than answers."

"Okay," Garcia said. "You shoot first."

"Has the NSA deciphered the code on the microdot?"

"That's above my pay grade, and even if I did I know, I couldn't tell you."

"Fine," Lorraine said. "What I really want to know is, why were the Russians so concerned about an old drug smuggling case that they sent Nick Volkov to dispose of the evidence and kill my family?"

"I'm sure that you have a theory about that," Garcia said.

"You bet I do. You and I both know that the Cuban government, on some level, facilitated drug smuggling from Central and South America for many years. The island was a safe house and a launching pad for boats and airplanes bound for our shores. Castro even had Tony de LaGuardia executed for involvement in the drug trade in 1989, even though he was a colonel in Castro's own Ministry of the Interior."

"That's common knowledge, Lorraine. De LaGuardia was almost certainly used as a scapegoat to protect the higher-ups, perhaps even

Castro himself. So, what's your theory on why the Russians got involved in Cuban drug smuggling?"

"I've been thinking about this for a long time. You know that I haven't always worked for the *Newport Daily News*. Years ago, I was an up-and-coming freelance journalist."

"I know," Garcia said. "I also know that the white spot on your temple—which is barely noticeable, by the way—is the reminder of a gunshot wound. You were grazed by a bullet in a roadside ambush in Colombia. That was in 1974, wasn't it?"

"Well, I see you've done your homework, Rene. You're exactly right. The terrorists could have easily killed me, but they held a pistol to my head and grazed my temple instead. Even so, the concussion knocked me out cold. After that I decided to come home and start a family, so I forgot all about the book I was writing. Do you know what my subject was?"

"I think I do. I've looked up a few of your old dispatches from Colombia and I'd say you were close to connecting Narco-terrorism and Soviet efforts to destabilize democratic governments in Central and South America."

"Yes," Lorraine said. "It is now accepted as fact that the Soviets actively supported Narco-terror groups like the Shining Path in Colombia, where the government couldn't stand up to the money and violence of the terrorists and chaos took over. So my question is why wouldn't the Soviets attempt to duplicate that success on American soil?"

"That's an interesting theory, Lorraine. But we can't blame our drug problem on Russian meddling. America is a very big country, and it's much more complicated than that."

"No," Lorraine said. "I'm suggesting something on a smaller scale than the whole country. Something more targeted, with a specific goal."

Garcia twisted toward Lorraine in his seat and said, "I'm listening."

"I've been sorting through old AP and UPI dispatches to try to make some sense of the drug problem back then, and I noticed an interesting thing. There was an epidemic of drug abuse and civil unrest in Washington DC that coincides exactly with the time frame of Ernesto's smuggling flights from Cuba. The *Washington Post* called it *Speedball Summer*."

"You're talking heroin and fentanyl," Garcia said.

"Yes," Lorraine said. "For a brief time, speedballs were incredibly cheap and available. Those users who did not die of overdoses became the worst kind of addicts and it caused a great deal of civil unrest in those blighted neighborhoods, with violent crime and riots on streets within sight of the Capitol dome. It was a national disgrace, and that is exactly the kind of chaos the Soviets loved to foment."

"Very good, Lorraine. I noticed that time line, too. But the agents who worked that case never figured out where the drugs were coming from. Some biker gangs and white supremacists were arrested transporting speedballs to the District of Columbia through Pennsylvania and Ohio, but there was no way to connect them to street dealers, who were most likely associated with the Black Panthers. That's a tough connection to make."

"But you're still investigating, aren't you? Can't you lean hard on Johnny? He must know something."

"Speedball Summer was all over when Johnny was born in 1976," Garcia said. "He was only Karl's messenger boy, so he's giving us some useful information about money laundering and other mischief that Karl was involved in later on, but not much else. The Bureau's field office in Baltimore is working on him since that's where Johnny lived before he was arrested in Florida. But to be honest, there isn't much interest in pursuing a thirty-year-old drug case."

"Can't you light a fire under the Baltimore office?"

"Lorraine, you might have noticed that the Bureau is a little overworked these days trying to prevent terror attacks and bank robberies. Consider that Karl Olson and his cohort, Arthur Johnson—who kidnapped Ali in the first place—are both dead. Nikoli Volkov has been banned from reentering the United States, and our government is trying to play nice with Cuba and Russia both right now. So, attempting to connect Karl Olson to skinheads, biker gangs, and speedballs in the slums of Washington DC a long time ago is not a priority."

"The Russians attacked us," Lorraine said. "That's what we're talking about and you know it. They used narcotics as a weapon to tear at the fabric of our society. That can't go unchallenged, even after three decades."

"You're right," Garcia said. "I doubt that following Johnny's trail is going to lead to a breakthrough in this case, but Karl might have been using him to dispose of old evidence. I suppose I could go down to Baltimore and see if something turns up."

"When?" Lorraine said.

"I might even fly down tomorrow," Garcia said, "and get it over with."

"Take me with you."

"What?" Garcia said. "I can't take a reporter along on an active investigation."

"I'll pay my own way," Lorraine said. "Consider me a confidential informant, since I may know some things about this case that you don't."

"That's pushing it, Lorraine. This could turn into a real shit show. My career is on the line and so is the integrity of the case I'm building."

"We're running out of time, Rene. Ali is in Europe right now searching for leads to Pilar. The NSA is never going to reveal what's on that microdot, so it's up to us to prove how the Russians were involved in this case. Until then, we're all in danger."

"How are you going to help?"

"I'm going to write about it."

"No offense," Garcia said, "but I think you're flattering yourself if you think the Russian intelligence services are worried that you're going to write about this case. You're not even on their radar. After all, you're just a housewife with a reporter job at a small-town newspaper. I'm telling you this because I like you, Lorraine."

"Damn it, Rene. You know that our government has been tamping down accounts of Russian espionage and meddling for decades. They want to make nice with the Kremlin, to pretend the Cold War never happened. It's all a backroom deal, all about business as usual. The only thing the Kremlin fears is our free press. Verifiable facts are their kryptonite, and an informed public is the only thing that can stop them."

"Okay, you win," Garcia said, raising his hands in surrender. "There are usually open seats on the first flight from Providence to Baltimore-

Washington International every morning. If you're at the gate, I don't suppose I can stop you from boarding with me."

Herr Rochat

Ali napped away much of the afternoon at the hotel.

"How are you feeling now?" Bernardo said after he had a light dinner brought up to their suite of rooms.

"Better," she said. "Except for a royal headache. And my hearing is still sort of muted and weird, like I'm underwater."

"Do you still think it was something you ate? Maybe we should see another doctor."

"No," Ali said. "I'm getting better. All I need is rest."

"Then come over here," he said, motioning her to the sofa. "Sit down and tell me what happened in Estonia. What town were you in?"

"It was Narva, in the eastern part of the country. In fact, you can see Russia from Rose's window."

"And Rose lives there alone?"

"Yes," Ali said. She was sitting close to him by then and her head fell on his shoulder when his arm was behind her. "She's all alone."

"What were you doing when you first felt ill?"

"Rose had gone to bed early and I was ready for sleep myself. But I sat down at the kitchen table with my laptop to check my mail. That's when it hit me, all of a sudden."

"Could you see Russia from Rose's kitchen?"

"Oh yes. It's right there across the river. I could see the lights of houses."

"Ali," Bernardo said, "is it possible that seeing Russia that close triggered some bad memories for you?"

"It sent a chill up my spine," she said. "But that wasn't what made me sick."

"Are you sure? After all, Nikoli Volkov has caused a lot of stress in your life. Maybe all that anxiety came to a head when you saw the lights of Russia across the river."

"No, something happened to me, Bernardo. I don't know what it was, but something physical definitely happened."

"Our minds can play tricks on us, Ali. It would be perfectly understandable if—"

"I'm not going crazy," Ali said. "I didn't imagine it. Something hit me hard enough that I had tingling in my ears. My vision even got blurry. Something did that to me, something real."

"I believe you," Bernardo said.

By then she had slumped against him.

"You're very tense," Bernardo said, rubbing her shoulder. "Just relax, Ali. We'll figure this out."

After a long silence she turned her face upward to meet his lips when she felt the breath of his whisper on her ear.

"You're a very beautiful woman," Bernardo said.

"Hold me tight," Ali said.

When the house telephone rang, Bernardo ignored it and kept his lips on Ali, moving slowly from her cheek to her neck.

"Take me to your bed, Bernardo."

"Not yet," he said. "I don't want this moment to end."

Ali did not hear the knocking at the door until it became insistent. Bernardo's hand was under her sweater when a voice outside the door said, "Police."

She pulled her sweater down but did not re-clasp her bra when Bernardo got up and went to the door.

"Bernardo, please don't open that door."

"It's okay," he said. "I can see uniformed officers through the peephole."

"*Guten abend,*" Bernardo said when he cracked the door. "What can I do for you?"

"I am Inspector Crelier of the *Stadpolzei Zurich*," a man in a suit said. "You are Bernardo Molina?"

"Yes."

"I will to speak to you now," the inspector said as he pushed into the room. "Who is this woman?"

"I'm Alicia Vasquez," she said, still sitting on the sofa.

"Your passports, please."

"What is this concerning?" Bernardo said.

"Passports, please."

"No," Bernardo said, "I won't advise my client to surrender her passport and neither will I. Not until my local attorney is present."

"Who is your attorney?"

"Herr Herbert Rochat."

"Do you know the whereabouts of Herr Rochat at this hour?"

"I imagine he is home or out to dinner," Bernardo said. "I'll call his cell phone."

"That won't be necessary. I have no time for charades, Mister Molina. Your conference with Herbert Rochat this morning is the subject of my examination."

"Why is that?"

"What was the purpose of your appointment with Herr Rochat?"

"Let's call him," Bernardo said. "He should be present before we continue this line of questioning."

"Herr Rochat has not been seen since you met with him this morning," the inspector said. "His meeting with you was the final event on his schedule before lunch with friends, but those acquaintances reported that he never arrived at their table."

"I don't understand that at all," Bernardo said. "Nothing Herr Rochat said when we met seemed out of the ordinary. I had simply requested his assistance in a banking matter on behalf of Miss Vasquez."

"Yet he has not been seen since," the inspector said. "His family is very concerned that he did not call or return home this evening. This is unusual in the extreme."

"My relationship with Herr Rochat is strictly professional, Inspector. In fact, I only met him in person for the first time today. I have very little to offer your investigation."

"That is yet to be determined," Inspector Crelier said. "I must ask you to remain where you are while we inspect your rooms to be certain that Herr Rochat is not present."

"I have no objections to a cursory examination," Bernardo said. "If it will help clear us as suspects, I'm all for it."

With that the uniformed men swept through the suite of rooms, looking under beds and in closets, until they were satisfied that Herr Rochat—or his body—was not there.

"Are you satisfied now?" Bernardo said when the men were finished.

"Not quite," the inspector said. "I will require the keys to your car in the hotel parking garage, please."

"The valet attendant has the key fob," Bernardo said.

"Very well," Crelier said. "Please do not attempt to leave this room."

"We're not going anywhere tonight," Bernardo said. "In fact, Miss Vasquez is feeling ill and needs to rest."

"I am sorry to hear that," the inspector said with a formal nod to Ali. "I will station one of my men at the door to be certain that you are not disturbed."

"You'd be better off using that man to search for Rochat," Bernardo said. "But if it is understood that he is here to protect the innocent, I'll be happy to have him there."

With that Inspector Crelier said, "*Guten Abend,*" and left their room.

Bernardo looked at his watch and then turned to Ali as soon as the door closed behind the inspector and said, "Are you okay?"

"No," Ali said, "I'm anything but okay. If something bad happened to Herr Rochat because of me—"

"We don't know what happened to Rochat yet, Ali. He might have been hit by a bus on the way home for all we know."

"No, you don't understand," Ali said. "I'm very afraid."

"I do understand," Bernardo said. "Remember that my father lost his life in the encounter with Nikoli Volkov and Karl Olson on Little Shady Key."

"I'll never forget that Vicente saved my life," she said. "But it is still okay to be afraid."

"It will be okay," Bernardo said, hugging her. "We'll figure this out. You should get some rest now."

"Please come lie with me, Bernardo."

"I will, but first I have to make a few notes about our encounter with Inspector Crelier."

"This is the beginning of something," Ali said. "Isn't it?"

"I'm afraid so," Bernardo said, holding her tightly. "What did Herr Rochat whisper to you before we left his office?"

"Herr Rochat whispered that the other allotment from Pilar's account had always gone to the Roman Catholic Archdiocese of Puebla de los Angeles, Mexico."

CHAPTER

6

Tuesday, March 22, 2005

Flight to Baltimore

It was cold and sleeting at the Providence Airport when Lorraine and Garcia checked in for the 5:30 a.m. flight to Baltimore.

"I'm never going to get used to this Rhode Island weather," Garcia said. "Freezing rain on the second day of spring just doesn't seem natural."

"This is typical," she said. "I'm used to it."

"Sure, but you grew up in South Carolina and lived in Tel Aviv and Paris when your father was our ambassador over there. Rhode Island must have been an adjustment."

"Listen, Rene," she said after they were seated on the airplane. "This isn't fair. You know everything about me and I don't know anything about you."

"Sorry, Lorraine. But I had to do a thorough background check on you as part of this investigation. And I must say, you've had a very interesting life."

"Why not level the playing field?" Lorraine said. "Tell me about yourself. Where are you from originally?"

"San Antonio," Garcia said. "I went to Texas A&M and spent six years in the Army. After that, I joined the FBI and got sent to Los

Angeles, where I spent most of my time chasing bank robbers. After a few years of that wild west show, I opted for a transfer to the Providence office."

"Why Providence?" Lorraine said.

"Because in Rhode Island we still go after gun-toting thugs, but we also get to arrest corrupt politicians, judges, and embezzler-bankers. It's nice to catch a big fish now and then."

"That's interesting, Rene. But you really haven't told me anything about yourself."

"Oh," he said, "and I met my wife in college. It has been an on-again, off-again thing. Right now, it's off."

"Thank you," Lorraine said. "But you should know that a woman would always want to hear more about how many children you have rather than how many bank robbers you've shot."

"No children," Garcia said. "Not yet, anyway."

"Thanks," she said, smiling at him. "Now I've got the picture."

They landed at Baltimore-Washington International an hour and forty minutes later, where Garcia picked up a rental car and drove them to a modern office building west of the city.

"It's bigger than I expected," Lorraine said when the guards at the main gate off Lord Baltimore Road cleared them to enter.

"This is one of our more active field offices," Garcia said as he parked the car. "They cover plenty of violent crime here. Not to mention, the offices of the CIA, the NSA, and about a hundred defense and intelligence contractors are in their area."

"No wonder they're dragging their feet on a thirty-year-old case."

"Exactly," Garcia said.

A young female agent came to the front desk to sign them in and escort them into the building. A black woman in a gray flannel pantsuit, she had short hair and a quick smile.

"I'm Nichelle Larson," she said. "The Miami office has Johnny Woods in custody and it's their case, but they asked us to investigate his background and activities here in Maryland. It landed on my desk six weeks ago."

"How long have you been an agent?" Garcia said as they walked to her office.

"About six months," Nichelle said. "So, what is your interest in this case, Lorraine?"

"Johnny tried to kill me, and most of my family."

"Oh," Nichelle said, "I'm sorry to hear that. But isn't it a bit unusual to bring a crime victim into the discussion of an active investigation?"

"Very unusual," Garcia said. "But this is an exigent circumstance. We might never crack this case without Lorraine's participation."

"Okay, here's what I've got," Nichelle said when they arrived at her cubicle in a large bullpen of agents. "We searched Johnny's apartment and seized most of his belongings. I can show you his stuff in the evidence vault if you want to see it, but these are the only items of interest so far."

She opened an envelope and dumped the contents—keys and a small black phone book—onto her desk.

"That's not much to work with," Garcia said. "How about his computer and cell phone?"

"There was nothing on Johnny's computer but links to porn sites," Nichelle said. "And we traced most of the numbers on his cell phone to hookers, bookies, and pizza delivery joints."

"I'm not the least bit surprised," Lorraine said.

"For other business he used prepaid credit cards," Nichelle said. "He did some business with a truck rental place in Glen Burnie, but the company said he was a model customer who didn't go far and always returned the trucks clean and full of gas."

"How about his little black book?" Garcia said.

"More of the same," Nichelle said.

"No friends or family?" Garcia said.

"None that I could find," Nichelle said. "Although he did call a cell phone somewhere in Odenton quite often, but I couldn't pinpoint the exact location."

"A girlfriend?" Garcia said.

"The only girlfriends were the kind that charge by the hour. Although there are a few phone numbers that are crossed out and others that we couldn't trace. Some of those came back as not in service, or they were combinations of area codes and numbers that made no sense at all."

"And the keys?" Garcia said.

"Miami sent us the key ring that went to his Mercedes," Nichelle said as she picked up the keys. "We found that these are the keys to his apartment, his mailbox, and several post office boxes. But these others are a mystery. Apparently they're the keys to another house or apartment and a padlock."

"Have you looked around Odenton?" Garcia said.

"Yes sir," Nichelle said. "But I can't walk up to every house and see if this mystery key fits."

"We might not have to do that," Garcia said. "Let's take a ride."

"Fine," Nichelle said. "I'll call the motor pool and check out a car."

"Not necessary," Garcia said. "I have a car out front. Bring Johnny's keys, and don't forget the little black book."

A half hour later they were speeding down the highway with Nichelle riding shotgun and Lorraine in the backseat. They were going ninety miles per hour when Lorraine said, "Do you always drive this fast, Rene?"

"It's one of the perks of the job," he said as he tossed his FBI credentials on the dashboard of the rental car.

It wasn't long before Nichelle said, "Take the next exit, please."

Then they were cruising a street of upscale retail stores with side streets of apartments and condominiums, while Nichelle instructed Garcia to make a series of left turns to box the area of the un-traced cell phone calls. Most of the units were in gated communities.

"This was probably all farmland a few years ago," Lorraine said.

"That's right," Nichelle said. "And there are so many housing units in this area that it's hard to pinpoint exactly where the calls were coming from."

"I thought you could triangulate the cell towers from a call and get a fairly accurate location," Lorraine said.

"Sophisticated criminals can dither their cellular signal and skip towers," Garcia said. "All it takes is a laptop computer and the right know-how."

Then he turned into a community of town houses and pulled up to the gate.

"Nichelle, take a look at Johnny's notebook," he said. "Read me the last four digits of one of those bogus telephone numbers, please."

"Nine-one-seven-three," she said.

Garcia typed the numbers into the keypad at the gate but nothing happened. Then he said, "Give me the next number."

"Two-six-three-two."

Nothing.

"Keep them coming," Garcia said, but none of the numbers opened the gate. So he drove to the next gated community, and the next, and repeated the process again and again.

"Open sesame," Garcia said, when the fourth gate they tried began to beep and open.

"I'm embarrassed," Nichelle said. "You made that look too easy."

"I've had a little practice at this game," Garcia said. "Johnny is too scatterbrained to remember codes and he was too sly to write them down where law enforcement—or other crooks—might find them. Security freaks often write down a bogus phone number as a way to remember pin codes and lock combinations."

"Okay, what do we do now?" Lorraine said. "Go from door to door to see if that key fits?"

"Not every door," Garcia said. "Let's pick the most likely units, like this one with the curtains drawn and no welcome doormat."

"It looks abandoned, but I'll give it a try," Nichelle said, and she got out of the car and walked up to the door. To her amazement, the key fit and the door opened.

"Great," Garcia said to Lorraine. "Let's go have a look."

They walked to the door, where Nichelle said, "Should we get a warrant before we go in?"

"You'll need some paper before the lab guys go over this place. Right now, let's see if anybody is home," Garcia said. Then he turned to Lorraine and said, "You stay here and don't touch anything."

The agents walked through all three floors of the townhouse with guns drawn and came back down to where Lorraine was waiting.

"Well?" she said. "Did you find anything?"

"Not much," Nichelle said. "The place is furnished and perfectly clean, but there are no personal items at all, no clothing or toiletries."

"So, what is this place?"

"This is a safe house," Garcia said as he holstered his weapon. "I'm betting that this is where Karl Olson stayed when he was in town, and God knows who else."

"The name on the lease might be bogus, but we ought to be able figure out who has been paying the bills," Nichelle said. "The utilities are all working, even the cable TV."

"That might not be so easy," Garcia said. "You'll probably find that the rent and all the bills are set up for automatic payment from a prepaid credit card. Johnny was most likely making a series of small payments into the credit card account with money orders, all untraceable."

"Smurfing?" Nichelle said.

"Now you're catching on," Garcia said.

"Okay, what's smurfing?" Lorraine said.

"A form of money laundering," Garcia said. "Criminals make a series of small cash or money-order payments into bank accounts or prepaid credit cards. The small deposits are not reported, so the funds are untraceable when they are spent."

"God bless America," Lorraine said. "Our banking system makes it easy for crime to pay."

"I'll get the crime scene guys to give this place a good going-over," Nichelle said as she reached for her cell phone.

"Wait a minute," Garcia said. "You can call in the lab crew later. We have another location to check out first."

"Where to now?" Nichelle said after she locked the door to the townhouse and they got back into the car.

"What's the address of that truck rental company Johnny used?"

"It's up in Glen Burnie," Nichelle said. "We did a thorough investigation there, but if you can pull another rabbit out of your hat, I'm all in."

Garcia drove up to Glen Burnie—too fast for Lorraine again—and stopped in front of the truck rental agency on the Arundel Expressway.

"Are we going in to talk to the manager?" Nichelle said.

"You already did that," Garcia said. "Let's try something else. How many self-storage places are there near here?"

"Dozens, I would guess," Nichelle said.

"Okay, we'll work out from this location in an expanding pattern and hit as many of them as we can."

"That could take all afternoon," Nichelle said.

"That's why they call this pounding the pavement," Garcia said. Then he turned to Lorraine in the backseat and said, "Are you okay back there?"

"Don't worry about me," Lorraine said. "I'm loving this."

They spent the next few hours driving to every self-storage facility within ten miles of the truck rental location with a quick stop at a diner for lunch. It was almost dark by the time they tried the code that hadn't worked at the townhouses, nine-one-seven-three, on a storage facility near I-95 and the gate opened.

"This is fun," Lorraine said, when Garcia drove into the facility, which appeared to be deserted.

"You know what to do," Garcia said to Nichelle. "If you get too cold, I'll come try the key."

"I'm too charged up to be cold," Nichelle said.

Garcia followed her with the car as she went from unit to unit, trying the key. It didn't take long to find a lock that snapped open.

"I hope there are no dead bodies in here," Nichelle said as Garcia got out of the car and helped her open the roll-up door.

"This is a lot better than that," Garcia said, when he clicked on his flashlight to illuminate an industrial rapid printing unit—like a copy machine on steroids—and cardboard boxes of printed materials.

"Can I come in?" Lorraine said.

"Sure," Garcia said. "Just don't touch anything."

"What is this?" Nichelle said.

"If I'm right," Garcia said, "this is the evidence that links the Kremlin to narcotics smuggling and distribution in Washington D.C. thirty years ago."

"The Russians?" Nichelle said, as she picked up one of the pamphlets from an open box.

"It was the Soviet Union back then," Lorraine said. "What does that say?"

"That's disgusting," Nichelle said as she threw the paper down.

"This is the most racist, vile stuff you'll ever find," Garcia said as he stood over the boxes of posters and pamphlets. "I've seen it before in case files from three decades ago, but we never knew where it came from."

"These people hate everyone," Lorraine said, when she looked over the papers. "Blacks, Jews, gays, and Mexicans. How can anyone with half a brain buy into this nonsense about a New World Order?"

"I don't know," Nichelle said as she clenched her right hand into a fist. "But I'd like to run into the asshole behind this shit when there are no witnesses around."

"You're too late," Garcia said. "I shot him dead two months ago."

Fresh Air and Sunshine

Ali and Bernardo were finishing a late brunch in their hotel room when Inspector Crelier knocked at their door.

"The situation has changed overnight," Crelier said. "Apparently Herr Rochat had another visitor after you left his office."

"Then we're free to go?" Bernardo said.

"Not so fast," Crelier said. "Rochat's notes of your meeting indicate he was investigating a possible fraudulent transfer of funds—significant funds, it would seem—from an account at Credit Suisse."

"That's correct," Bernardo said. "We were going to meet again today."

"In that case I would have you speak with our financial crimes office. I will take you to our headquarters for an interview."

"No," Ali said. "First, tell me about this other visitor to Rochat's office."

"That matter remains under investigation," Crelier said.

"That's not my problem," Ali said, standing up. "I'm concerned for my safety and for Bernardo as well, and I'm not talking to anybody until you tell me who this mystery visitor was."

"You're in no position to issue demands, Miss Vasquez."

"Miss Vasquez is not without rights here," Bernardo said. "I have already contacted the American embassy and informed them of our situation. On their recommendation I have arranged for the international law firm of Bar & Karrer AG to represent Miss Vasquez and myself in this matter. I will require that a team of their attorneys be present for future discussions."

"That's just going to take more time," Ali said, tugging on her robe as she sat down. "If you really want to find Rochat quickly, let's stop playing games. Who was with Rochat after us?"

"Very well," Crelier said, pursing his lips before continuing. "A nearby shopkeeper's surveillance video captured two men leaving Rochat's office less than an hour after you. One of the men appears to be Herr Rochat."

"Now we're getting somewhere," Ali said. "Tell me, did Rochat appear to be going willingly with this other man?"

"Ali, be careful," Bernardo said. "I know where you're going with this, but please don't make statements that might implicate yourself."

"Thank you for that," Ali said. "But I only want to help the inspector find Herr Rochat before it's too late. So, I'll ask again, did the other man seem to be helping Rochat into a waiting car?"

"Now you would do well to heed the advice of your attorney," Crelier said.

"Because I'm right," Ali said. "This man was helping Rochat, who was partially incapacitated—perhaps ill—wasn't he?"

"How would you know that, Miss Vasquez?"

"Because that man was Nikoli Volkov," she said. "Three months ago he tried to force me into a van in Baltimore. He is an agent of the Russian government, and a Taser is his favorite weapon to disable victims."

"You will have to explain that statement very carefully," Crelier said.

"Miss Vasquez does not wish to make any further statements," Bernardo said. "She has given you the information you need to find Herr Rochat under duress and against the advice of her attorney."

"Please listen," Ali said. "You can't guarantee our safety here. I'm sorry if something happened to Herr Rochat, but you're dealing with a professional who was able to kidnap a prominent lawyer from his office at high noon on a busy street with no eyewitnesses other than a chance video snippet. No good can come if Bernardo and I remain in Zurich while Volkov is on the loose. Please allow us to leave your country immediately."

"I can support that," Bernardo said. "You should contact the chief of security at the American embassy to verify that my client has been the victim of past crimes perpetrated by Volkov and others aligned with the Russian Federation. You are exposing Miss Vasquez to extreme danger by holding her in Zurich."

"We, too, are professionals," Crelier said. "I can guarantee you safety, of that I am certain."

"Your own men will be the first to get hurt if Volkov gets to us," Ali said. "I feel terrible about Herr Rochat, but there is no need for others to suffer. Just allow us to leave and let our lawyers sort this mess out."

"I can guarantee my client's cooperation through the attorneys at Bar & Karrer," Bernardo said. "There is no need for Miss Vasquez to remain in Zurich."

"Perhaps," Crelier said, softening his tone. "I will escort you to the prosecutor's office. If he clears you, you will be permitted to depart from there."

"Good," Bernardo said. "I'll call the valet to bring my car around to the front door."

Ali gathered her things and dressed quickly. Then Inspector Crelier and four armed men escorted her and Bernardo down to the lobby, where the valet handed the keys to the sleek Mercedes-Benz to Bernardo.

"It is a short distance to the prosecutor's office," Crelier said. "You will follow my car."

"Certainly," Bernardo said. "Give me a moment to put our bags in the trunk, please."

Ali and Crelier stood on the sidewalk while Bernardo went to the rear of the Mercedes with his suitcase and Ali's small bag. It was a fine day in Zurich, and many people were walking near them on the Badener Strasse, enjoying the fresh air and sunshine.

Ali knew something was wrong as soon as Bernardo raised the lid on the trunk.

"Inspector…" Bernardo said.

Later, Ali would wish that she had not followed Crelier to the rear of the car where Herr Rochat's ashen face was aimed vacuously at the sky with his elegant fingers curled to his chest—where they had lost their grasp on life.

Ships Passing

Lorraine and the two FBI agents were sitting in a coffee shop across the street from the storage unit when Nichelle said, "Okay, would you mind telling me what this is all about?"

"They called it Speedball Summer," Garcia said. "One of the worst drug epidemics in American history."

"Sure," Nichelle said. "I'm hazy on the details but I've heard that case mentioned as an example of how illicit drugs can rip apart the fabric of society. I'm confused because the Miami office didn't say anything about an old drug epidemic. They only told me to investigate Johnny's connection to a kidnapping case and a recent home invasion in Florida."

"Did they mention the bomb that destroyed an Anthem Airways flight on the runway in San Juan?" Lorraine said. "And nearly killed everyone onboard?"

"They didn't say anything about that," Nichelle said.

"They wouldn't," Garcia said. "Because the higher-ups at the Bureau are convinced that Puerto Rican separatists bombed that flight."

"Whom do you suspect?" Nichelle said.

"I'm focusing on the Cuban intelligence services," Garcia said. "And the Kremlin, since that was who Karl Olson and Johnny were working for. I suspect that the bomb was meant to eliminate the prime witnesses to some Russian crimes."

"The Russians?" Nichelle said.

"That's right," Lorraine said. "My husband was the pilot on that flight, and he and I were both in the house when Olson, Johnny, and a Russian agent tried to kill us all. That couldn't be a coincidence."

"But how do the Russians fit into all this?"

"That Russian state security officer was sent with Olson to steal the evidence of past crimes and kill my family in the process," Lorraine said. "That's all the proof I need. The Kremlin was definitely involved."

"Okay," Nichelle said. "If all that is true, what does that racist bullshit we found in that storage unit have to do with drugs in the District of Columbia?"

"When you get back to the office, look up the case files for Speedball Summer," Garcia said. "The agents who worked the case never found the source, but the mules who got nabbed with that particular drug combination on I-80 in Pennsylvania and Ohio were all members of biker gangs, or neo-Nazis and white supremacists."

"Wait a minute," Nichelle said. "Are you trying to tell me that the KKK took off their white sheets and came into the toughest neighborhoods in DC to deal drugs with the Black Panthers?"

"Exactly," Garcia said. "If I'm right, Johnny's boss was a former CIA man who was working for the Russians to create chaos in the United States. His game was to stoke hate and discontent inside any group with a grudge against the rest of us. He probably provided money and support—even weapons and drugs—to fringe elements of all persuasions, as long as they hated someone else and had total disdain for our government and the rule of law."

"Olson was using that racist propaganda to make nice with skinheads and biker gangs so they would be his drug distribution network," Lorraine said. "At the same time he was stoking their bigotry and hatred. That sounds like perfect propaganda to me."

"Right," Garcia said. "And I'll bet you both a steak dinner that some of those boxes in the storage unit contain a very different flavor of propaganda, stuff that would appeal to disenfranchised blacks."

"Wait a minute," Nichelle said. "What you're alluding to sounds incredible. That would make the safe house we found—and that racist crap in the storage unit—evidence of a possible Russian attack on our country."

"That's exactly what it was," Garcia said. "When you put all this all together, it proves that the Kremlin bombed our nation's capital with narcotics. But some very powerful people don't want this investigation to see the light of day, so be careful. It is altogether possible that the KGB people responsible for Olson's past activities are now very senior and powerful in the Russian Federation. My theories are just speculation at this point, so I suggest that you collect the evidence and present the local facts as you see them and leave the deep conspiracy angle to me."

"It sounds like you want me to have all the credit for discovering the safe house and the racist material," Nichelle said.

"I do," Garcia said. "You were tasked with investigating Johnny's activities in Maryland. I just pointed you in the right direction."

When a small fleet of cars pulled into the diner's parking lot, Nichelle went outside to talk to her supervisor and the additional agents he had brought to the scene. Then they went across the street to seize the material and the printing press in the storage unit.

"That was nice," Lorraine said.

"What?" Garcia said.

"You gave Nichelle credit for a big break in this case."

"She's going to be a good agent," Garcia said. "She'll be on the radar of the top brass after this, and I'm betting that girl will shine."

"You know, you're not the tough guy you appear to be," Lorraine said. "You're a nice man, Rene."

"Don't go telling people that," Garcia said. "To do this job I need to maintain my intimidating image."

"You're not intimidating to me, Rene."

"That's okay," he said. "Listen, I have to stay in Baltimore tonight to help Nichelle wrap this up. You can stay with me, if you'd like."

"Rene, are you making a pass at me?"

"You're a very attractive woman, Lorraine."

"I knew you were going to be trouble, Rene. Those eyes."

"I'm only human."

"Well, I'm flattered," Lorraine said. "It's been a long time since a man as young and handsome as you took an interest in me. But you'd better take me to the airport for my flight home now."

Leaving Zurich

The mood in the state prosecutor's office was tense and unsettling. "We all knew and respected Herbert Rochat," Stefan Parmelin said when Ali, Bernardo, and Inspector Crelier were seated before his massive mahogany desk. "No lawyer in this city had a higher respect for the law or a greater understanding of monetary crimes. That is why it is hard to accept that he has been murdered and that our police have apparently bungled the investigation."

"We have followed procedures with exactness," Inspector Crelier said.

"Nonetheless, the body of our esteemed colleague has appeared—as if by magic—in the very first place you should have looked."

"I personally examined the trunk of that car two hours after Rochat was reported missing," Crelier said. "We are still investigating how the body was placed there afterward, but we have learned that the valet on the nightshift was sleeping heavily, as if he had been drugged. It may have been possible for someone to take and return the keys while he was unconscious."

"You needn't concern yourself with such details any longer," Parmelin said. "I am taking over this investigation."

"As you wish," Crelier said, nodding—almost bowing—his head.

"Now, as to you, Miss Vasquez," Parmelin said. "It may interest you to know that Rochat had already contacted us, as was his usual practice, concerning the possible theft of funds from your family account. He always kept this office apprised when dealing with any suspected international money laundering case."

"Then you know that Miss Vasquez and I certainly did not wish that any harm would come to Rochat," Bernardo said. "He was our ally in this matter."

"That's right," Ali said. "I feel terrible that such a nice man may have been hurt because of me."

"That is understood," Parmelin said. "And it seems that you also have a powerful ally in your government, in that two security officers from the American embassy will arrive here shortly to escort you to the airport."

"Bertram," Ali said to Bernardo. "Lorraine told him I was going overseas. He must have been looking out for me."

"So, you are allowing us to leave Switzerland?" Bernardo said. "Without conditions?"

"Yes, you are free to go. All I ask is that if you intend to return to Zurich, please notify me personally so that I can make the appropriate security arrangements."

"I'm not planning to come back any time soon," Ali said. "But if I do you'll be the first to know."

"Also, I trust that you will cooperate fully with my investigation," Parmelin said.

"You bet I will," Ali said. "Sooner or later, someone has to catch Volkov and make him pay for all his evil deeds."

"If I determine that this Volkov you speak of is the perpetrator, I will do my best to bring him to justice, Miss Vasquez. But I must tell you that the European Court of Human Rights is under great pressure from several amnesty organizations not to grant extradition in such cases. Unfortunately, their liberal zeal for the rights of criminals over the rights of victims—which may be well-meaning in a manner that is beyond my comprehension—often plays into the hands of men like Volkov."

CHAPTER

7

Wednesday, March 23, 2005

The Seller

The Swiss Air flight from Zurich arrived in Miami precisely on schedule at 1:20 p.m., after which Bernardo took Ali straight to his condo on Key Biscayne. She was standing in the sunshine on the balcony overlooking the dock and his speedboat when she turned on her cell phone and called Lorraine.

"Hello, Ali," Lorraine said. "The good news is that the seller has collected his money for the painting we bought for you. I'm flying down with Connor and Nathan this evening so we can all go up to West Palm Beach tomorrow, if you'd like."

"You're bringing Nathan, the son I haven't met? What happened to Bennett?"

"Bennett has a bit of a legal problem right now, so he can't leave Rhode Island."

"What sort of problem is that? Does it have anything to do with me?"

"Actually, it does involve your situation. But I'd rather give you the details tonight, in person."

"Listen, Lorraine, I'm in no mood for guessing games right now. I just got off a last-minute flight from Switzerland since my lawyer in Zurich was murdered right after our meeting. And something dreadful happened to me at Rose's apartment in Estonia that left me with a nasty headache. So just tell me, please."

"What?" Lorraine said. "Bertram told me you had some trouble in Zurich, but what exactly happened in Estonia?"

"I'm not even sure what it was," Ali said. "But I can't shake the headache or the nagging suspicion that Nick Volkov had everything to do with it."

"Volkov?" Lorraine said. "You saw Nikoli Volkov?"

"No, I didn't see him at all. But I could see lights in Russia from Rose's apartment when I first felt ill. And before he died my lawyer in Geneva told me that some Russians stole a lot of money from Pilar's account. That's Volkov, Lorraine."

"I'm so sorry," Lorraine said. "But at least you're back on US soil, where he can't get to you."

"You don't know the half of it yet," Ali said. "But I wouldn't be so sure about Volkov. I don't think he's going to give up until he gets my picture of Ernesto."

"In that case I might as well tell you now, the FBI has your snapshot and the microdot. Bennett picked it up after the fight in Ransom's house and didn't tell us."

"Oh my God!" Ali said. "Now you tell me? How did the FBI get it?"

"That's what I'll explain tonight, Ali. Just sit tight. We'll be there in a few hours."

"I don't think I can wait," Ali said. "I've got to talk to that kid you got the new painting from. What was his name, Jaime? Give me his cell phone number, please."

"I will but remember that he doesn't know you. Please wait for me and Connor."

"I'll try to do that," Ali said, to end the call with Lorraine. But she dialed Jaime's number while she was still standing on the balcony and arranged to meet him in a few hours.

All I need is a car, Ali thought.

Bernardo was at his desk at one side of his living room when she went inside. Ali waited for him to finish a phone call before she asked him the question.

"Bernardo, can I borrow a car?"

"Of course. Take the roadster if you can drive a stick."

"Thanks," she said, taking the key. "I'll be back in a few hours."

"That's fine. We'll have dinner when you get back."

"Thanks," she said, turning to leave.

"Ali," Bernardo said, "where are you off to in such a hurry? I thought you would want to rest after all you've been through."

"I can rest later," she said. "Right now, I might find some answers in West Palm Beach."

"I'll come with you," he said, leaning forward as if to stand at his desk.

"No, only I should go," she said, kissing his forehead and sitting him back down. "This boy might be more willing to talk with a woman alone."

"Then be careful," Bernardo said. He pulled her close and kissed her mouth. "I want you all to myself tonight."

Jaime

The Mercedes roadster would have been a joy to drive under other circumstances. But as Ali sped along the Florida Turnpike her mind was only on Pilar.

Jaime was sitting with a friend when she walked into Combat Cuisine and he eagerly waved her toward their booth.

"How did you know it was me?" Ali said as she sat with them.

"That was easy. You look just like Pilar."

"You've never seen Pilar. You're too young."

"You're right," Jaime said. "But I've studied every known picture of her. The ones in the art history books are all black and white, but they say she had brilliant green eyes—just like yours."

"That's nice of you to say," Ali said. "Who's your pal?"

"I'm Ricky," the kid with the Mohawk, tattoos, and piercings said. "I'm the one who actually sold the painting to your friends."

"I see," Ali said. "So, when the seller came by to get his money, you must have gotten his name and address for a receipt, right?"

"Nope," Ricky said. "We just take our cut and hand the seller their cash. That's the way it works here."

"That's okay," Jaime said. "I was sitting right here when Ricky closed the deal. I know where we can find the guy."

"Really? How is that?"

"He had grit under his fingernails and rough hands—like a mechanic—and he was wearing a work shirt from the muffler shop on Okeechobee Boulevard. You know, one of those places that does tires, brakes, and exhaust stuff. His name is Gus, if you can believe the name on his shirt."

"Good job," Ali said, patting Jaime on the arm. "Maybe you can show me where this shop is."

"Sure," he said, with a wide smile. "They're probably open right now."

"I'll come, too," Ricky said.

"Sorry," Ali said, "I'm driving a two-seater today. But I'll bring this handsome fellow right back, okay?"

Jaime followed her out of the restaurant and hopped into the roadster with his backpack. Ali glanced at him when she could on the city streets and saw that he seemed to be enjoying the ride like a puppy.

"You can put your backpack behind the seat," Ali said.

"I'm okay," Jaime said, holding the pack in his lap.

"I get it," Ali said. "It's your security blanket, isn't it?"

"Yeah," Jaime said. "This is a really cool car."

"I know. It belongs to my friend, Bernardo."

"Your boyfriend?"

"Maybe," Ali said. "Too soon to tell. So, how do you know so much about Pilar Vasquez?"

"I'm doing my thesis on her," he said. "At least, I will, if I ever finish my degree."

"Okay, but why Pilar?"

"I don't know," he said. "I guess because nobody else seems to understand her."

"But you do?"

"Oh yeah," Jaime said. "I totally get her stuff."

"That's good to know," Ali said.

She followed his directions and parked at the curb across the street from the shop. The service bay doors were open, and they could see men in blue work uniforms around the cars on lifts.

"That's him," Jaime said, when a man came out front and looked around the parking lot, wiping his hands on a rag.

"How can you tell from here?" Ali said.

"His build," Jaime said. "And the way he walks. I sort of notice those things."

"Okay," she said. "Let's just sit here a while."

They didn't wait long before the cars came down off the lifts and the overhead doors closed one by one.

"Looks like quitting time," Jaime said.

"Right, and probably a good time for me to meet Mister Gus. Wait here, Jaime."

The shop was empty when she walked into the service bay from the waiting area, but she could smell the pungent aroma of burning herb through the back doors, which were still wide open. The men were outside in the back lot leaning on the wall when she came around the corner.

"We're closed, miss," a man said. "Better come back tomorrow."

"Are you Gus?" she said.

"Yeah," he said. "What do you need?"

"I'd just like to have a word or two with you."

"Are you a cop or something?"

"Definitely not," Ali said.

"Then how about a hit," he said, revealing the lit joint he'd been holding at his side.

"I don't think so," Ali said. "Just a few words, if you don't mind."

"Sure," he said, handing the joint to another man. "I always got time for a good-looking gal who ain't a cop."

"Okay," Ali said, around the corner from the others. "Tell me about the painting you sold to me at Combat Cuisine."

"Hey, I didn't steal that fricking picture," Gus said. "My aunt Margie gave it to me."

"Easy does it," Ali said. "I just want to find out where the painting came from, that's all. Can I talk to your aunt Margie?"

"Not unless you got a really good long-distance line. She's dead."

"Oh, I'm sorry to hear that," Ali said. "Do you have any idea where she got it?"

"Hell if I know," he said. "Her condo in Boca Raton was full of that sort of stuff, old pottery and blankets and shit from Mexico. I threw most of it in the trash."

You've got to be kidding me, Ali thought.

"How do you know those weren't priceless artifacts?" Ali said. "Do you even know why she was interested in Mexico?"

"That old biddy was a college professor," he said. "She was always going to Mexico to look down a volcano or something."

"Which college was she at?" Ali said. "It would really help me to know that."

"I don't know," Gus said. "I'm into fast cars and rock and roll. I don't give a crap about that other stuff."

"I get that," Ali said. "Could you at least tell me Margie's last name?"

"Gustafson," he said. "Just like me. What did you think it was?"

"Got it," Ali said. "Thanks, I might come back to see you again, if you don't mind."

"Anytime," Gus said. "We'll go have a drink, okay?"

Ali sprinted back to the roadster and surprised Jaime with a sloppy kiss on his cheek.

"You're a beautiful damn boy," she said, shaking his shoulders. "This is the best damn day of my life."

"Cool," Jaime said.

"You're coming to Miami with me," Ali said, as she let go of him and revved the roadster's powerful engine. "I want you to tell my friend Lorraine everything you know about Pilar Vasquez."

"Way cool," Jaime said, taking a piece of wrapped hard candy from his pack. "Want a Jolly Rancher?"

The Plan

Connor, Lorraine, and Nathan flew down to Miami International Airport that evening, where they picked up a rental car and drove to Key Biscayne.

"Look who I brought home," Ali said when they arrived at Bernardo's condo and saw Jaime.

Lorraine introduced Nathan to Jaime and Bernardo while Connor handed the painting they had bought at Combat Cuisine to Ali, along with her envelope of cash.

"Here it is," Connor said. "We spent $350 of your money for this and here's the rest."

"Thanks," Ali said, looking at the painting. "This is amazing. I can't believe I'm holding something that Pilar painted not that long ago."

"This is probably only about five years old," Jaime said, standing at her side. "Look at the exposed canvas on the back and you'll see that it is still bone white. It hasn't aged at all."

"That doesn't mean Pilar painted this," Nathan said. "What makes you think it isn't just a knockoff?"

"Just look at the strokes, her choice of palette, and the way she laid the oil on the canvas," Jaime said. "And the mountains and stars in the background are classic Pilar Vasquez style."

"I'm no art critic," Connor said. "But Pilar ran with Fidel Castro and Che Guevara and painted murals that glorified the Cuban Revolution, so why would she paint a radiant cross of Jesus beaming down on a kid with a burro? That doesn't add up for me."

"It will all make sense after I pass on Herr Rochat's parting words in Zurich," Ali said. "We were on our way out of his office when he whispered that money had been drawn from Pilar's bank account for the Roman Catholic Archdiocese of Puebla de los Angeles, in Mexico. And the man who sold this painting got it from an aunt's apartment that was full of Mexican art."

"Bingo," Connor said. "Now we're getting somewhere."

"Let's sit down," Bernardo said, motioning them into his living room, which overlooked Biscayne Bay. "Are you hungry? Perhaps a glass of wine?"

"None for me," Nathan said. "Ali, can I borrow that painting for a moment? I want Jaime to tell me how he can be so sure it is a Pilar original."

The two boys moved to a lamp near the windows with the painting while Bernardo brought out a bottle of Chardonnay and a tray of Brie and crackers, followed by fruit and a glass of cranberry juice for Connor.

Then Ali calmly told Lorraine and Connor about the meeting with Herbert Rochat, but when she came to the part where his body was found in the trunk of Bernardo's car, her composure failed and tears came.

"That poor man," Ali said. "I keep thinking about his family waiting for him to come home, and not knowing."

"It's not your fault," Lorraine said.

"Maybe not," Ali said. "Rochat certainly knew the risks of following illicit money to the Kremlin, but I should have told him that the Russians attacked me in Estonia. And I foolishly told Rose that I was going to Zurich next—so they were on to me and the threat was imminent. He should have known that."

"Tell us what happened in Estonia," Lorraine said.

"I know it sounds crazy," Ali said. "But they beamed something across the river and into Rose's apartment that made me so sick I could hardly stand. I'm still getting over it and I'm afraid that my hearing might never be the same."

"What you're describing sounds like a sonic attack," Connor said. "Bertram is pretty tight-lipped about Russian espionage technology, but he does admit that they have some sophisticated ability to use highly directional sound waves to snoop on us and even to harm us, if they want to."

"I believe that, and more," Ali said. "The buzzing in my brain didn't stop until I put two solid walls between me and the window. Even then I had to take down a copper ornament that was vibrating."

"Oh?" Connor said. "That is interesting. Did you know that early in the Cold War the Russians gave our ambassador in Moscow a wooden eagle to mount in his office? The tiny transmitter hidden inside had no power source, since it was activated by bombardment with radio waves of a specific frequency from outside the embassy. It picked up secret conversations for years until we discovered what was going on."

"I guess they could have been using that ornament in Rose's apartment as a reflector of some kind," Ali said. "It was directly in line with the hallway and the window looking to the Russian side of the river."

"Ali," Lorraine said. "Do you suppose that Rose knew about all of this?"

"I don't know," Ali said. "It's frightening to think so, but she did make a phone call as soon as I arrived. So I don't know."

"It sounds to me like Rose's apartment was configured as a trap," Connor said. "My informed guess is that they intended to completely disorient and incapacitate you with that attack so you couldn't resist when they came to drag you across the river to Mother Russia."

"That's a terrifying thought," Bernardo said, putting his hand on Ali's forearm. "Thank God they weren't successful."

"Amen to that," Lorraine said. "But the best thing you can do is move on. So why don't you tell us how this painting ended up in an apartment in Boca Raton?"

"Actually," Ali said, "the man who put the painting on consignment at Combat Cuisine came by it when he was cleaning out the apartment of a spinster aunt who had passed away. He didn't tell me much—I don't think he knew his aunt very well—but he did say that her name was Margie Gustafson and that she was a college professor."

"That's not much to go on," Lorraine said.

"That's where Jaime comes into the picture," Ali said, motioning him to sit next to her and Bernardo. "As a student himself, he was able to get into the university computer system and find a lot of information about Aunt Margie."

"It was easy," Jaime said. "She was a professor in the geosciences department at Florida Atlantic University so all her research papers and reports are still online, including the annual field trips she led to Popocatepetl."

"The active volcano in Mexico?" Connor said.

"Dad," Nathan said, "how do you know about volcanos in Mexico?"

"I know because volcanic dust turns jet airplanes into gliders if you fly into the plume even hundreds of miles downwind. We keep pretty close tabs on eruptions and Popocatepetl has been a real nuisance for years."

"So, what are you thinking?" Lorraine said. "Do you suppose that Aunt Margie bought Pilar's painting on one of those trips?"

"That sounds reasonable to me," Ali said.

"Right," Connor said. "Except that you can buy trinkets and art as soon as you step out of the airport in Mexico City. What makes you think the painting came from near Popocatepetl?"

"Just remember what Herr Rochat told me," Ali said. "Pilar's account was sending money to the Archdiocese of Puebla de los Angeles, which is southeast of Mexico City in the shadow of Popocatepetl."

"There's more," Jaime said. "I can tell you where Professor Gustafson probably stayed when she visited Mexico. A town called Arroyo de Riendo is mentioned in all her reports. I think she liked to stay there."

"Arroyo de *what?*" Nathan said.

"Arroyo de Riendo," Jaime said. "Laughing Brook."

"Connor," Ali said. "What do you think now?"

"I think we're going to Mexico," Connor said. "I'll call Ransom and ask if we can borrow Old Snort for a few days."

"Wait," Bernardo said. "Who is Ransom and what is this Old Snort?"

"Ransom is my brother," Lorraine said. "He was Connor's wingman in the Navy."

"Right," Connor said. "And Old Snort is the twin-engine airplane he let us use to visit Smuggler's Hole in the Everglades where we found the wreck of Ernesto's airplane. Snort is an antique but a very solid machine."

"When would you propose to do this?"

"Right away," Connor said. "Ali and I are on reserve with Anthem Airways right now, but in April we'll be flying on the schedule again. So we need to get this done."

"So you're going to jump in an old airplane and fly to Mexico, just like that? Why not buy an airline ticket?"

"Actually, Ali and I could just flash our airline credentials and get seats to Mexico City," Connor said. "But I want to be flying our own plane so we can screw out of there on a moment's notice if things get dicey. Besides, I like to fly Old Snort."

"You'll get used to the way the Laird family operates," Ali said, smiling at Bernardo. "They don't screw around."

"True," Lorraine said. "But we'll need a cover story. If I remember correctly, the drug cartels are fairly active in the mountains southeast of Mexico City. We can't just barge in and announce that we're looking for Pilar Vasquez."

"We?" Connor said. "I was planning on just me and Ali for this mission."

"I don't think so," Lorraine said. "I'm going with you."

"Dad," Nathan said, "when will you be coming back?"

"This shouldn't take but a day or two on the ground in Mexico," Connor said.

"I agree," Lorraine said. "In and out, quick and dirty. Otherwise, we're asking for trouble."

"Then can I go?" Nathan said. "I don't have to be back at school until Monday."

"Definitely not," Connor and Lorraine said in unison.

"But I cracked the code on the paintings. I deserve to go with you on this one."

Connor turned to Lorraine and said, "He has a point."

"I guess so," Lorraine said, settling the matter.

"How many seats does this Old Snort have?" Bernardo asked.

"It's set up for freight right now," Connor said. "But we can put up to six seats in back plus two pilots up front."

"In that case, I'll clear my schedule for the rest of the week," Bernardo said, looking at Ali.

"That would be nice," Ali said.

"What about me?" Jaime said. "Can I go?"

"I'll have to think about that," Connor said.

"*Yo hablo Espanol*," Jaime said. "I can blend, and I know how to find Pilar's paintings. That might be helpful."

"That's true," Lorraine said.

"You'll need your passport," Connor said.

"Right here," Jaime said, patting his knapsack. "Don't leave home without it."

"Okay," Connor said. "We'll drive down to Ransom's Landing on Little Shady Key early tomorrow morning. Agreed?"

"That sounds good," Lorraine said. "I've already reserved us two rooms at the hotel in Miami for tonight. We can head over there anytime."

The Laird contingent was gathering their gear and getting ready to leave Bernardo's condo when Ali leaned close to Lorraine to whisper,

"Please take Jaime off my hands tonight."

"Sure," Lorraine said. "Jaime can stay in Nathan's room at our hotel tonight."

CHAPTER

Thursday, March 24, 2005

El Comandante

Bernardo had suggested that they meet for breakfast at a café near his office in Little Havana before driving to Little Shady Key.

"Do you come here often, Bernardo?" Lorraine said as they sat.

"Not that often," Bernardo said. "Vicente used to meet his *companeros* from Havana at these tables nearly every morning. These days I might stop in for coffee now and then just to keep in touch with the old ones, but I don't often have the time."

Breakfast was *bistec a caballo* for Connor, pancakes for Nathan, and breakfast tortillas for everyone else, after which Lorraine surprised them all with a slight change in the plan.

"Bernardo, is it okay if Connor and Nathan drive down to Little Shady Key with you and Ali? I'd like to stay in Miami for a few hours to get some background material for my book."

"Sure," Bernardo said, "but Miami is my city. Perhaps I can help you with any information you might require?"

"It's nothing, really. I'd just like to get some of the local flavor for the book. Jaime knows the local scene and he can keep me company."

"Are you sure you don't want me to stay with you?" Connor said.

"You need to get the ball rolling with Ransom's airplane, don't you?"

"Right," Connor said as he handed her the keys to the rental car. "Whatever you're up to, be careful, Peaches."

When the others left the restaurant, Lorraine and Jaime sat at their table and watched Bernardo's Mercedes disappear down the street.

"Where are we going now?" Jaime said.

"Nowhere," Lorraine said. "Have another cup of coffee."

"How long are we going to sit here?"

"Not too long, I hope. Why don't you tell me how your family came to America?"

"I think my grandfather came over alone when he was very young to attend Catholic school here in Miami. The rest of the family came a few years later."

"That's interesting," Lorraine said. "Was he in the Pedro Pan Airlift?"

"I suppose so, but we don't usually tell people that. I mean, what does it matter? We're here now and I'm an American kid."

"But you're interested in Pilar Vasquez, who was a figure in the revolution that drove your family from their home."

"Yeah, I guess it's like a horrible train wreck—you can't look away. Besides, I'm happy we came to America. So how long are we going to sit here?"

"As long as it takes," Lorraine said. "Sometimes a journalist just needs to follow her instincts."

"What are we waiting for?"

"Not what, but who," Lorraine said. "Keep talking and have another coffee."

Then a few minutes later she said, "Here we go," when an old hombre came in and sat with another old man at a table in the back of the café.

"Who is that?" Jaime said.

"That's Paco," Lorraine said. "The boyhood friend of Bernardo's father in Havana, Fernando Castro."

"And who is he sitting with now?"

"If we're lucky," Lorraine said, "that's someone very important to our story, someone who is very interested in Pilar and her daughter. Let's go say hello."

By the time they walked across the restaurant to the small table where the two old men were quietly speaking, Lorraine was reasonably certain that her instincts had been true.

"*Buenos dias, Senor Castro,*" she said. "It is good to see you again, although I had expected that you would be back in San Juan by now."

"*Buenos dias,*" Paco said. "I'm going back tonight, thank you."

"Am I correct in assuming that this is *Capitan* Tejera?" Lorraine said. "*Buenos dias, senor.*"

"*Si, yo soy Tejera,*" Paco's companion said. *"Buenos dias."*

"I apologize for the intrusion," Lorraine said. "May we join you briefly?"

Paco nodded yes, and Jaime pulled two chairs alongside the table after Lorraine introduced him as a friend.

"Anything you can tell me about the time Ernesto and Pilar spent in the Sierra Maestra would be appreciated, *Senor* Tejera. Even small details might help Alicia find Pilar."

"I should not have come here," Tejera said. "I meant no harm, and only wished to see Alicia one final time, even if from afar."

"She was an infant when you last saw her?" Lorraine said.

"Yes." Tejera nodded. "I was there the morning she was born."

"Tell me, *Senor* Tejera, do you recall the date?"

"*Si*, that was January 11, 1972."

"Who else was present?" Lorraine said. "Was there a birth certificate?"

"Besides myself, only Ernesto and a midwife were present," Tejera said. "So other than an entry in the daily report of my garrison's activities, the only record of Alicia's birth was in the notebook I kept for myself, which I presented to Vicente Molina several months ago, after he first contacted me."

"Did you list Ernesto Fuentes as the father in your report and notes?"

"No," Tejera said. "They had only been together seven months before Alicia was born."

"That's interesting," Lorraine said, her eyes wide with the revelation. "Can you tell me when Pilar came to the Sierra Maestra?"

"That was the twentieth of June. I remember the day precisely because I traveled to Havana to bring Pilar to the *hacienda* where Ernesto had been waiting."

"So, Pilar was with Ernesto seven months, more or less?" Lorraine said. "Then Alicia was born?"

"*Si, mas o menos.*"

"That changes everything," Lorraine said. "Are you sure?"

"Yes. Pilar was not well when I took her from the headquarters of the Revolutionary Police. The trip to the Sierra was difficult for her and required two days in the back of an army truck."

"So, you picked up Pilar in Havana, not at the *Presidio Modelo?*"

"That is correct. She had been held in Havana by the Revolutionary Police for several months before I took her to the Sierra, and she was not well."

"Not well?" Lorraine said. "What do you mean?"

"She had been beaten," Tejera said, lowering his eyes.

"By whom?" Lorraine said.

Tejera only shook his head no. Then he looked up and said, "You must understand that I was with Camilio Cienfuegos for the victory at Yaguajay, never Fidel. When Camilio was murdered, I had no choice but to take an obscure post in the Sierra. I was never a part of Fidel's apparatus."

"*Tomalo con calma,*" Paco said. "Take it easy, my friend. We all did what we had to do to survive."

"We hoped Pilar would be the one," Tejera said. "We hoped for so much from her. Then to see her that way—"

"Thank you," Lorraine said, standing to leave. "You've been quite helpful, *Senor* Tejera. I won't trouble you again. *Buena suerte.*"

Lorraine and Jaime were in the rental car when he turned to her and said, "Why did you tell him we wouldn't bother him again? I have a million questions."

"There are no answers for those questions," she said. "None that you and I would understand, anyway."

"But what will we tell Ali?"

"Nothing," Lorraine said. "Not a word. Those men were betrayed by their own dreams, and we should leave them alone."

Little Shady Key

"When you called me yesterday, I thought you were kidding," Ransom Calhoun said after Bernardo's Mercedes pulled up to the hangar at his airstrip on Little Shady Key. "You want to go to Veracruz? With guns?"

"We're going hunting," Connor said.

"It's illegal to bring guns into Mexico. They don't screw around."

"That's why we need your help, shipmate. I'll have to borrow some long guns from you, too."

"Hi, Uncle Ransom," Nathan said.

"Nate, you're too old to call me uncle," Ransom said as they shook hands. "And please tell me you're not going on this escapade. You're supposed to be the sane one in this family."

"Hello, Ransom," Ali said when he gave her a hug. "This is Bernardo Molina, Vicente's son."

"Welcome," Ransom said, taking Bernardo's hand. "Your father was a great man."

"That's very kind of you," Bernardo said. "With your help we may be able to complete his final mission for Ali."

"You're asking a lot," Ransom said. "But I've already made a few calls, so maybe we can work something out. Let's get out of the sun over at Marta's place."

When the screen door at Marta's little restaurant slammed shut behind them, she came out of the kitchen to greet the group, wiping her hands on her apron before hugging Ali.

"It is so good to see you again," Marta said. "Sit down, I'm pressing *cubanos* for all of you."

"This is an interesting place," Bernardo said. "Is this all yours?"

"Most of it," Ransom said, waving toward the runway and his house. "Marta runs the restaurant and the cabanas for me, and the boats belong to the guides. I don't charge them much to use my docks because they bring business to Marta."

"A nice arrangement," Bernardo said as Marta set cold bottles of beer on the table with a ginger ale for Connor.

"So," Ransom said, raising his beer. "What is in Veracruz?"

"Actually, we're going a little past the coast," Connor said, "to Arroyo de Riendo. Ever hear of it?"

"What?" Ransom said, slamming his bottle to the table. "That's the last place in Mexico you should go. Stay in Veracruz, Connor. Better yet, forget about Mexico and go back to Rhode Island."

Nathan said, "What could be so bad about a place called Laughing Brook?"

"Ha!" Ransom said. "For starters, the brook is nothing more than a tiny spring spitting hard water from the base of a volcano. Other than that, there's nothing there but farmers and sleepy *cantinas* full of mushroom hunters."

"Mushrooms?"

"*Setas magicas,*" Ransom said. "Magic mushrooms. You know, the psychedelic kind. They're legal in Mexico."

"Forget the mushrooms," Ali said. "I think Pilar might be there."

"Didn't you learn anything from the last time you went looking for Pilar?" Ransom said. "Maybe you should go look at the bullet holes in the walls and ceiling of my house, just to refresh your memory."

"You didn't patch the holes?" Connor said.

"No, I like them," Ransom said. "It's fun to show them to friends when they come over."

"Ransom, don't be rude," Ali said. "Remember, Bernardo's father lost his life in that fight."

"That's quite all right," Bernardo said. "I'm not offended. But I'll pass on a tour of the battlefield if you don't mind."

"Listen, you don't need to go to Arroyo de Riendo," Ransom said. "I used to know the chief of police there. Let me make a call."

"Please don't mention Pilar to the chief," Ali said.

"Why not? The chief is the only person in that dump you can trust."

"Ask the chief about the airport," Connor said. "It looks abandoned but it might still be useable."

"Connor, I'm not going to let you fly my sister into that godforsaken place," Ransom said. "Where is she, anyway?"

"Mom stayed in Miami to check on some things for her book," Nathan said. "Now how about showing me these bullet holes, Ransom?"

Newport

"Uh-oh," Bennett said when he and Natalie walked out of Rogers High School and saw Rene Garcia's dark blue SUV parked behind his old Jeep in the student parking area.

"He's got you cornered now," Natalie said. "Want me to scram so you boys can talk?"

"Hell no, you might have to drive my Jeep home if he arrests me."

"He's not going to arrest you, dummy. You haven't done anything."

"Actually," Bennett said as they walked toward Garcia, who was out of his SUV and waiting for them. "I took a toke of weed with the guys at Tuckerman's while you were working for Doc Monroe yesterday afternoon."

"First of all, that was stupid," Natalie said. "And second, the FBI isn't going to arrest you for that."

When they reached Garcia, the FBI man said, "What am I not going to arrest you for, Ben?"

"Uh, nothing," Bennett said.

"I was just kidding," Natalie said.

"Is that so? Didn't I hear you say Ben did something stupid?"

"Wow, you've got really good hearing," Bennett said. "For an old guy, I mean."

"Thanks, Ben. Sound carries a long way in cold air. Now, where are Connor and Lorraine?"

"I think they went to Miami."

"Okay," Garcia said. "Are they with Ali Vasquez?"

"Yeah, I suppose so. They were going to see her."

"Right. They're trying to find Ali's mother, aren't they?"

"Yeah, and I'm sort of pissed I had to stay home this time. They took Nate instead."

"Okay," Garcia said. "So, you and Nathan send text messages back and forth all the time, don't you?"

"Uh—actually, not so much."

"I get that," Garcia said. "My brother is a bore, too. But if Nathan happens to tell you where they are and who they're with, you're going to call me right away, aren't you?"

"Gee, I don't know about that."

"Come on, Ben," Garcia said. "We have an understanding, don't we?"

"Yeah, but it wouldn't be cool to rat on my family."

"We're all on the same team, Ben. Nick Volkov is the bad guy, remember?"

"Why don't you talk to my grandfather? He knows all about that Russian stuff."

"I already did talk to Bertram. I was at your house with him for a few hours today and he told me where everybody was."

"Really? Then why are you asking me stuff you already know?"

"I just like to see how you answer, Ben. That way I'll know if you ever lie to me."

"That kind of sucks," Bennett said. "I tell you everything I know and you never tell me anything. That's a screwy setup."

"Fine," Garcia said, opening the door to his SUV. "Here's something you might not know—Ali and Vicente Molina's son were in Zurich two days ago and the lawyer they met with came to a very untimely end."

"Really? You mean he died? You don't think they did it, do you?"

"No, I don't and neither do the Swiss police. That's why they let them go back to Miami."

"Jeez," Bennett said. "That's really something. Who do you think—?"

"Nikoli Volkov," Garcia said. "You're a smart guy, Ben. You ought to realize that my job is to protect your family even when they go off doing things they shouldn't. Nathan might tell you something that your parents would never say, so help me out by telling me where they're going next, okay?"

"I don't remember the Spanish name," Bennett said, "but I think it was a place in Mexico called Smiling River or Laughing Brook or something like that."

Little Shady Key

"Hey, Mom," Nathan said as soon as Lorraine came in the door at Ransom's house, where the group was huddled over charts and papers spread across the dining table. "How much do you weigh?"

"That's not a polite question for a lady," Lorraine said. "Why do you ask?"

"I'm helping Dad plan our flight to Mexico and my job is to total up the weight of the passengers and our luggage."

"In that case put me down for one-fifty," Lorraine said.

"How about you, Jaime?"

"One-thirty," he said. "And all I have is my knapsack."

"You won't need much," Nathan said. "We're only going to be there two or three days."

"Hi, Peaches," Connor said when he looked up from the huddle. "How did you make out in Little Havana?"

"Okay," she said. "When are we going to take off on this expedition?"

"Early," Connor said. "Did you learn anything new this morning?"

"No, Fernando Castro and a friend came into the restaurant and we talked to them for a while, that's all."

"Fine," Connor said, having learned years earlier that his spouse would give him the details when she was ready to do so. "Let me show you what we're going to do."

Lorraine leaned over the chart while Connor pointed to their route.

"We'll leave here early in the morning and fly direct to Veracruz, eight hundred and seventy nautical miles west in about five and a half hours. That puts us sixty miles off the coast of Cuba and thirty miles off the Yucatan for part of the flight."

"That's a lot of water to cross," Lorraine said, eying the wide expanse of blue on the chart that was the Gulf of Mexico.

"We can divert to Cuba or the Yucatan," Connor said, "if we really have to."

"If you head for Cuba, just drop me off in the Gulf," Ali said. "I don't think that Pilar Vasquez's daughter would be well received in Havana."

"Good point," Lorraine said. "Wouldn't it be safer to fly over land to New Orleans and Texas and then down to Mexico?"

"That would be a two-day trip," Connor said. "Old Snort isn't a jet, so we'll only be going about one hundred and sixty miles per hour."

"Peaches, I agree with you," Ransom said. "Old Snort started life as a military transport so she has long-range tanks, but going straight across is pushing it—not that the Great Captain Connor Laird would worry about such details."

"There's a big high-pressure area up north," Connor said. "By tomorrow it will be over the Carolinas with a big clockwise circulation that will give us tailwinds all the way to Veracruz."

"Theoretically," Ransom said. "But if that tailwind doesn't come through for you, land at Merida in the Yucatan, not Cancun."

"Why is that?" Ali said. "Cancun is closer."

"We have friends in Merida," Ransom said.

"Which is somewhat of a concern for me," Bernardo said. "Your friends appear to be very well connected, Ransom. Hunters are normally advised to apply for visas to bring firearms into Mexico months in advance with the assistance of a licensed guide, yet you were able to make arrangements in a few hours on your Blackberry phone. How is that?"

"Easy," Ransom said. "Your guide is the chief of police in Arroyo de Riendo, and your visas will be waiting in Veracruz. Trust me."

"Trust comes hard to attorneys," Bernardo said. "We prefer proof. I have to know what I'm getting myself and my client into, and frankly, a man with your questionable connections and a base at an isolated landing strip in the Florida Keys makes me wonder."

"Sure, I had a few adventures," Ransom said. "But I've settled down now, and even in my wild days I was never convicted of anything worse than a speeding ticket or two."

"Only because you pull that war hero routine every time you get in trouble," Lorraine said.

"Your brother is a war hero," Connor said. "Being the last American airman shot down over North Vietnam is a big deal. You'd know that if you weren't so busy protesting the war at Columbia University at the time."

"We all did what we had to do," Lorraine said. "To your point, Bernardo, we never ask my brother about his little peccadilloes even though any illegal activities would be devastating to our father's reputation. But if he and Connor can get us into Arroyo de Riendo with a reasonable cover story, I say we go and try to find the person who created what appears to be a Pilar Vasquez original oil painting."

"Very well," Bernardo said. "What time are we leaving?"

"Zero-four hundred," Connor said. "I'd like to fly up to Arroyo de Riendo as soon as we clear customs in Veracruz so we have plenty of daylight while we try to find a little-used airstrip in the mountains."

"Make sure you bring plenty of cash," Ransom said. "You'll need US dollars to buy fuel for the trip home and I've promised my customs guy in Veracruz one thousand bucks. Also, you'd better believe that the chief at Arroyo de Riendo will be looking for a generous tip."

"What are we going to do when we get there?" Jaime said.

"Bernardo and I are going hunting," Connor said. "That will get us a good look around outside of town. The rest of you are going to hang in town like tourists, scoping out the *cantina* and the market where Aunt Megan might have bought the painting."

"There are less than one hundred houses in Arroyo de Riendo," Ransom said. "So you might be able to walk around and meet some of the locals. If Pilar was ever there, they might tell you."

"If you know so much about the town, why aren't you coming with us?" Jaime said.

"I might have a little problem with the *Federales*," Ransom said.

"That's a good point," Ali said. "If the Mexican state police have problems with you, how do you have so much pull with the local chief of police?"

"You'll see," Ransom said.

CHAPTER

Friday, March 25, 2005

Flight to Veracruz

Hours before the first light of the day would show in the east, Connor stood alongside the airplane and said, "Last chance to back out, boys and girls. Do you all have your passports ready?"

"We're all set," Lorraine said.

"Fine," Connor said. "Let's get aboard."

Nathan and Jaime had stumbled straight from their beds to the airplane. They were already sleeping again in the seats at the back of the cabin when the group came aboard and duck walked up the aisle below the low ceiling.

"Renville!" Connor said. "Rise and shine, boys."

"Are we there already?" Nathan said, without opening his eyes.

"No, there are some things you need to know before we get started. This is important, so all of you please listen carefully," Connor said, sitting side-saddle on the armrest of a seat. "There is an inflatable life vest for each of you. I want you to put them on now and keep them on as long as we are over water."

"Is this really necessary?" Lorraine said.

"Simply a precaution," Connor said. "Ali and I will be wearing ours up front as well. Pulling straight down on the lanyards will inflate the vest. There is also a manual tube you can blow into if it comes to that."

"This is getting a little scary," Nathan said. "You never had us do this on the airline."

"This old crate is no Boeing, Nate. It will get us there okay, but it's smart to take every reasonable precaution along the way. For instance, that yellow bundle you're resting your feet on is our life raft. Your job will be to toss it out the door if we end up in the water. You'll have to pull all the lanyard all the way out and give a hard jerk at the end to inflate the raft, but for God's sake don't inflate the thing inside the airplane or we'll never get it out the door. Do you understand?"

"Got it, Pop."

"Good. You'll also see that the lanyard is connected to the airplane near the door to serve as a tending line once the raft is inflated. Don't cut it until we are all in the raft as the raft will blow downwind much faster than the airplane and we certainly don't want to lose it."

"I'll help," Jaime said.

"Very good," Connor said, as he pulled the cabin door closed.

With everyone belted into their seats, Connor started the engines, sending a pleasing vibration though the airframe. Ransom's airstrip was unlighted so he turned on the wing landing lights when he back-taxied to the far end of the pavement.

"Flaps set?" Connor said when they were turned around for takeoff. "Controls free, mixtures rich, props full forward."

Then he pushed the throttle levers forward and the radial engines roared and throbbed with power. Old Snort gathered speed gradually at first until Connor lifted the tail wheel off the runway and the landing gear struts extended as the wings gained lift. Then they were flying and he turned over the Gulf of Mexico to climb to the west.

They soared above a ghostly layer of scattered low clouds, barely visible by the moonlight. The cockpit was awash with the soft glow of the instrument and map reading lights, but the cabin was a dark cavern where the passengers were dozing or gazing out the windows. Soon the lights of Key West were just a memory.

"Isn't that Cuba?" Bernardo said, leaning into the cockpit to get

Connor's attention.

"Havana," Connor said. "About ninety-five miles away."

"It looks closer."

"Distances can be deceiving at night, Nardo."

"Ha," Bernardo said. "My father used to call me Nardo, only he used to roll the R a bit."

"I'll remember that," Connor said. "What are you thinking about when you see those lights?"

"I'm thinking how pissed Angela will be if she has to bail me out of a Cuban jail cell," Bernardo said. "So let's stay far away from that place."

"You got it, Nardo."

About an hour into the flight they started seeing dull flashes to the south—the yellow flickering of lightning embedded in clouds.

"Let's hope we get some daylight before we get near any of that crap," Connor said.

"I know," Ali said. "Without radar we're like blind men groping around out here in the darkness. How is our tailwind holding?"

"It's beautiful right now," Connor said, tapping the portable GPS mounted on his control yoke. "Twenty-two knots. We're all set if that holds up."

When the sun finally peeked over the horizon behind them, it illuminated a wall of clouds ahead of them in a golden glow.

"I don't think we can climb over that," Ali said. "But it looks like we can scoot around to the right a bit and avoid the buildups."

"We can try that," Connor said as he twiddled the heading knob on the autopilot twenty degrees to the right.

"What's going on?" Lorraine said when she leaned into the cockpit between the pilots.

"There's some weather up ahead," Connor said. "We'd like to go around it."

"You can fly in clouds, can't you?"

"Yes, but without weather radar on this airplane we can't see the thunderheads through the more benign clouds. We'll just have to work harder to avoid them, Peaches."

"I thought you checked the weather before we left?" Lorraine said.

"I did," Connor said. "And I said it was good, not perfect. We'll be okay but everybody should tighten their seatbelts back there. It might get a bit bumpy soon."

They were flying in and out of white cumulus clouds at eight thousand feet when Ali said, "I don't see a way around this."

"Right," Connor said, "We can go under and avoid the heavy rain or go up and try to pick our way around the worst of it. What do you think?"

"Up," Ali said.

"Fine," Connor said, switching off the autopilot. "You have the flight controls. Take her up to angels twelve. That's all we can do without oxygen."

At twelve thousand feet Old Snort was still not completely out of the mist, but in the clear air between the broken clouds they could see towering cumulus clouds ahead.

"Pick a light spot and head for it," Connor said, but the clouds around them grew darker. Soon the mist was thick and gray and when the sudden turbulence rocked their wings he said, "Don't worry about holding altitude, Vasquez. Just keep us right side up."

"Whoa," she said. "This isn't good."

"Just roll with it, Vasquez," Connor said when the clouds turned black and greasy. "This old crate can take it as long as we don't pull the wings off by fighting with the controls."

In the heart of the storm it was black as night and Old Snort was jolted up and down as if pounded by a giant jackhammer.

"If you see a light spot, head for it," Connor said.

"Over there looks better," Ali said, looking to the right.

"Easy," Connor said, when she banked the wings. "Standard-rate turns and keep the controls coordinated."

A few seconds later the angry clouds spit Old Snort out into clear, smooth air. The sky ahead had a deep blue hue and a rainbow appeared against another nearby thunderhead, which they easily avoided.

"Please do something with this," Lorraine said when she tapped Connor on the shoulder and handed him an airsickness bag.

"No problem," Connor said as he cracked open the sliding window at his shoulder far enough to toss the sack out into the slipstream.

"Hey, Pop," Nathan said a few minutes later. "Where's the bathroom on this plane?"

"I told you to go before we took off," Connor said.

"That was before you gave us that E-Ticket ride. I have to go now."

"Fine, there's a bucket and plastic bags behind the rear seats."

"A what? A bucket?"

"This isn't first class on the airlines, Nate."

"That sucks."

"Embrace the suck," Connor said. "You volunteered for this mission."

Newport

When Bennett came out of the house in the morning, he was greeted by a dark blue SUV parked in the driveway behind his Jeep.

"Hi, Agent Garcia. Am I under arrest?"

"Are you feeling guilty about something again, Mr. Laird?"

"No, but if you put handcuffs on me now, I won't have to take my math test today, that's all."

"No such luck, Ben. Is the ambassador home?"

"Sure, come on inside," Bennett said, leading Garcia toward the back door.

They entered through the kitchen and found Bertram reading in his favorite chair by the fire in the living room.

"Good morning, Rene," Bertram said. "Have you learned anything new?"

"I have some information for you," Garcia said. "Our man in Mexico City sighted their visas to go hunting in Puebla State."

"Hunting?" Bertram said. "That seems odd. I don't believe Connor has hunted in decades. But Lorraine was somewhat evasive about their final destination—you know how paranoid she is about wiretaps—that's why I called you so late last night."

"I'm glad you did, Ambassador. At first glance the paperwork for their visas appeared to be in order, but our man in Mexico City smells something fishy. The initial applications to bring firearms into Puebla should have been filed months ago, but he can't locate them."

"That is somewhat distressing," Bertram said. "I'll call Lorraine and advise her not to make the trip today."

"It may be too late, Ambassador. Late last night Connor filed a flight plan to Veracruz, so they may be en route to Mexico already."

"Then I will advise her to leave soon after they land in Veracruz," Bertram said. "By the way, where were they going to hunt?"

"The destination listed on their visas is a sleepy town in the shadow of a volcano, a place called Arroyo de Riendo."

"Perhaps our embassy in Mexico City could intercede on their behalf," Bertram said. "I'll make some calls to Foggy Bottom."

"That would be a good thing," Garcia said. Then he turned to Bennett and said, "You'd best get going, Ben. You don't want to be late for that math test."

"How can I sit in school when everybody is in Mexico with guns? I want to help."

"They'll be all right," Bertram said. "I'm sure your mother will call off this trip after I talk with her. Now, off with you, young man."

"I miss all the good stuff," Bennett said as he left.

"Ambassador, you should make those calls right away," Garcia said after Bennett was outside. "The Mexican Federal Police won't go near Arroyo de Riendo without a battalion of marines to back them up."

Welcome Wagon

Ali made the landing at Veracruz by greasing the main wheels onto the one long runway at General Heriberto Jara International Airport shortly after noontime. Then they all had to wait until the customs man came aboard and took a seat behind the cockpit, with his briefcase open on the floor between the pilots' seats.

Connor sat sideways and presented each of their passports and paperwork listing the particulars of their two rifles—not mentioning the pistols hidden behind inspection panels in the left wing. The customs man only glanced at their paperwork with no apparent interest until Connor dropped an envelope fat with cash into his briefcase. The man didn't look at the envelope and his expression never changed when he stamped their papers, closed the cover of his briefcase, and stood up.

"Welcome to Mexico," he said as he handed their passports back to Connor.

"That was easy," Ali said when they walked toward the terminal to hit the bathrooms and grab lunch.

"Getting out might be a little trickier," Lorraine said.

"That's why I'm having the fuel tanks topped off here," Connor said. "If we have to leave Arroyo de Riendo on short notice, I want to have enough fuel to get to Texas nonstop, either McAllen or Brownsville."

"Good idea," Bernardo said.

After they stretched their legs Connor herded the group back to the airplane.

"Dad," Nathan said, "why didn't you exchange dollars for pesos to pay for the gas? Didn't they want the local currency?"

"Here's something they might not have taught you at the Eliot School of International Affairs," Connor said. "Wherever you go, Ben Franklin is king. Everybody wants American C-notes."

"I agree," Bernardo said. "I haven't found a place yet that isn't happy to take US dollars."

"How long will it take to get to Arroyo de Riendo?" Jaime said.

"Another two hours," Connor said. "Are you having second thoughts?"

"No, sir!" Jaime said. "This is the coolest thing I've ever done."

"Good for you," Ali said. "We're glad to have you with us. Aren't we, Connor?"

"Sure," Connor said, looking skyward. "Absolutely."

When they climbed back aboard Old Snort, they took the same seats.

"At least we won't need these things anymore," Lorraine said as she stuffed her life vest under the seat.

Connor started the engines and they took off to the west, flying over a gritty industrial area that quickly gave way to cultivated fields of crops beneath the wings.

"Are you sure we're in the right place?" Nathan said as they flew over the farmland. "I was expecting tumbleweeds and cactus in Mexico."

"Take a look," Connor said, pointing ahead of the airplane, where the jagged cone of a barren mountain rose above the fields.

"Wow," Nathan said after he craned his neck to see. "That sure looks like a volcano."

"Right," Connor said. "That's Popocatepetl."

"I thought you said it was active? I don't see any smoke."

"El Popo has been sleeping since last year," Jaime said. "I found a paper that Professor Gustafson published about the last smoke-show in January 2004."

"That must have been her last visit to Arroyo de Riendo," Lorraine said.

"Right," Ali said. "All we have to do now is find the town."

"How small is this place?" Bernardo said. "Isn't it on the map?"

"It's small for sure," Connor said. "But Ransom told us where to look."

They flew along the base of the volcanic cone where the barren dry lava flows met the fertile soil below until they sighted a small cluster of buildings. From the air the town was nearly a perfect square of stone houses, all with walled courtyards.

"That has to be their airport," Ali said, pointing to a flat gravel strip alongside the one road that led down off the mountain and appeared to connect the town to the outside world. "There are no facilities but you can see a few airplanes on the ground."

"Right," Connor said. "But those airplanes all look wrecked. They might be here only because they were in no condition to take off after landing on this strip."

"That's a comforting thought," Lorraine said. She had crept up to the cockpit and was kneeling between the pilots for a better view.

"I suppose a windsock would be too much to ask for?" Ali said as Connor circled the runway. "Which way will you land?"

"The wind won't make much difference," Connor said. "It looks like there's a slope to the runway so we'll land uphill, toward the town."

Then he turned to Lorraine and said, "Better tell everyone to buckle up back there."

"Good luck," Lorraine said, backing out of the narrow space between the pilots' seats.

"Relax, Peaches," Connor said. "This is what I do. It's a piece of cake." Then he said to Ali, "Put the gear down please, and give me a notch of flaps."

As it was, the wind was blowing directly across the runway, so Connor crabbed in and straightened the airplane at the last moment, dropping the upwind wing to land firmly on one wheel. Then he parked Old Snort in a corner of the strip and shut down the engines.

The silence was deafening when they climbed out of the airplane and stood behind the wing. With the cold volcanic cone towering nearby, the fields of crops all around them were the only sign of life.

"Now what?" Nathan said, holding his phone to the sky. "I don't suppose they have cell towers around here."

"We could walk into town," Jaime said.

"I don't think that will be necessary," Connor said. "We flew low enough over the houses that somebody will be out here soon."

"This looks like the welcome wagon now," Bernardo said, pointing to a plume of dust coming from the town.

"Right," Connor said, when they could see that the dust was being kicked up by two pickup trucks driving toward them at high speed. "It could be the local constabulary. Let me do the talking."

When the trucks were on them and scratching to a halt on the loose gravel, they saw that each truck was full of armed men, looking more like rabble than police.

"This isn't good," Bernardo said when the men surrounded them with automatic weapons at the ready and began pulling anything that wasn't bolted down out of the airplane.

"I'm the pilot," Connor said. "Who's in charge here?"

"Not you," someone said, and the men all laughed.

"Have a seat," a man with a florid face said. He wore a sleeveless Harley Davidson of Las Vegas shirt and carried a sawed-off shotgun. "You're not going anywhere for a long time."

Lorraine ducked into the shade under the left wing and the others followed until they were all sitting and lying on the gravel, while the men removed their luggage from the cabin of the airplane and picked through the bags, tossing their belongings on the ground. When they had finished scouring Old Snort, the men stood nearby, smoking and laughing.

"What now?" Nathan asked, but the men ignored him.

They didn't have long to wait before another pickup truck came speeding out of the town. The truck came straight at them and swerved menacingly close to the tail of the airplane before screeching to a halt behind the left wing. As soon as it was stopped, one of the armed men handed the cash they had collected from the group into the cab of the truck.

"Que tenemos aqui?" a dark young woman said. *What do we have here?* When she leaned out of the truck's cab to accept the cash, they saw a buxom woman in a halter top and Ray-Bans, with her curly black hair sticking out the back of a New York Yankees baseball cap.

"Es esta Arroyo de Riendo?" Connor said, standing up. "We're supposed to meet our guide here."

"Like I give a shit?" the woman said. "Come over here."

Standing alongside the truck—once he got past the sight of her ample breasts, which were barely contained by her halter top—Connor saw that she was wearing a shoulder holster and cradling an automatic assault rifle on her lap. The muzzle was pointed his way and her left hand was on the pistol grip. The sawed-off shotgun resting near her feet and a spare pistol on the dashboard told Connor that they had arrived in a tough neighborhood.

"What are you doing in my town?" she said.

"We're going hunting. Like I said, we're supposed to meet our guide."

"Are the women going hunting?"

"They might," Connor said. "Mostly they just want some down time in a warm place."

"Who's this little one?" the woman said, pointing her chin at Jaime.

"Jaime is my nephew," Bernardo said, with his arm around the boy's shoulders. "I brought him along to meet Alicia, my fiancé."

The woman pulled her Ray-Bans down and said, "Bullshit."

"All right," Connor said. "Who are you?"

"I'm the chief of police and these are my men, and you are terrible liars. You sat under the wing where your contraband is stashed. That was a rookie mistake."

"What contraband?" Connor said.

"Let's find out," she said, handing the red-faced man a screwdriver. "Here you are, Martillo, you know where to look."

The man shoved Lorraine and Ali aside and crouched under the left wing. When he opened the inspection panel and reached inside, he found two pistols and brought them to the woman.

"What were you going to hunt with these?" she said.

"We had visas to bring weapons into your country," Connor said.

"Two rifles and two shotguns," she said. "Not handguns. You're lucky the customs men in Veracruz were on *siesta* when you came through. Let's go now. Put your stuff in the back of the truck. Men in the back and ladies in here with me."

When she opened the cab of the truck, they saw that there were steel plates bolted to the inside of the doors with cut-outs so she could shoot through the outer skin without raising the muzzle of her assault rifle to the window.

"Where are you taking us?" Lorraine said.

"I'm taking you hunting," she said. "I'm Leona, your guide. Ransom Calhoun arranged this shit show."

Arroyo de Riendo

They drove through fields of corn and sugarcane that ended against the adobe walls of the town, which was cut by narrow streets paved with stones between more adobe walls. Through some gates they could see that the walls formed courtyards for small houses with livestock, children, and laundry drying on lines. There were very few cars.

"This town is like a fortress," Nathan said, sitting in the bed of Leona's pickup truck.

"The walls are for the *lobos*," Jaime said. "The wolves used to run wild in little towns like this with the fields all around."

"The wolves are mostly gone," Connor said. "But if you lived out here in the middle of nowhere, you'd want walls, too."

The snowcapped cone of Popocatepetl loomed above the town,

where the main street was only slightly wider than the rest, with a paved square around a dry fountain. There was a *cantina* with outside tables on one side, across from a small church next to a walled compound that had barbed wire atop the ramparts.

A guard opened the chain-link gate as they approached.

"What is this place?" Ali said after the trucks were inside the walls of a large courtyard.

"*La Guarnicon*," Leona said. "This is my garrison, but you can call it our city hall. Some of my men live over there and over here is the jail, where you will be staying. But first, come into my office."

"You're putting us in jail?" Bernardo said.

"Not really," Leona said, carrying her rifle and their cash from the truck. "We don't have much crime in Arroyo de Riendo, so we often use these rooms with bars on the windows for special visitors. You may find it more comfortable to leave the doors open at night."

"Isn't there a hotel we could stay at?" Lorraine said.

"They have rooms at the *cantina*," Leona said. "But you'll be safer here with me."

"Why do we need protection," Connor said, "if there is no crime here?"

"We prevent crime from happening."

"Right," Connor said. "It looks like your army outnumbers the civilians."

"My men cover a large territory outside these walls," Leona said as she led them into a building at the front of the garrison that contained the post office, a bank, and a pharmacy. Her office was in the back of the building.

"Just to be clear," Bernardo said, as they found seats around Leona's desk. "Are we in custody?"

"Roam the streets of the town during the day as you wish," she said. "But don't venture beyond the outer walls without my permission and an armed escort."

"I'll need to go check on our airplane from time to time," Connor said. "And I'd like your assurance that we can depart whenever we wish."

"You're already a pain in my ass," Leona said. "So, feel free to get in your little airplane and take off anytime. But first, there is the matter of your fees."

"You have almost all of our cash," Connor said.

"Of course," Leona said, setting their C-notes on her desk and moving some piles aside as she ticked off the services. "Two large for hunting licenses, four large for guide services, two large for lodging, and two large for transportation."

"Ten thousand bucks?" Connor said. "We already wired you five grand from Florida before we set out on this boondoggle."

"That seems like a fair amount to me," Leona said. "I'll hold the rest of your cash in my safe, as a precaution. There will of course be a departure fee."

"Departure fees?" Ali said. "How much are we talking about?"

"That depends on what you depart with," Leona said. "You obviously came here to get something. There will be a tax on the value of the goods you take home."

"We're not here for drugs," Bernardo said.

"That's hard to believe," Leona said. "Many of our guests are here to hunt mushrooms."

"Magic mushrooms?" Nathan said.

"That's what they call them," Leona said. "But they don't do much for me. I like tequila."

"Don't some people come here to study El Popo?" Jaime said.

"A few," Leona said. "There was a professor who stayed with me a few times. She was a bore, but some of her students were fun to have."

"Margie Gustafson?" Jaime said.

"Yes, that might have been her name," Leona said. "Why do you care about her?"

"Just a coincidence," Connor said. "Jaime was her student, once. We're here to go hunting. Do we start tomorrow morning?"

"Yes, but what are you hunting for?"

"We'd like to do some wing shooting," Connor said. "The quail hunting is supposed to be very good here, isn't it?"

"It is good," Leona said. "But you didn't bring those big game rifles for birds."

"If we see a deer, we'll take it."

"I see," Leona said. "I'll play along with you, but I warn you, don't piss me off. Now, let's go over to the *cantina* so you can all get shit-faced and tell me what you're really hunting for."

Newport

"May I come in, Ambassador?"

Bertram was home alone when Rene Garcia came to the front door. The two men went to the kitchen to talk.

"How do you take your coffee, Rene?"

"Black, thanks."

"Now," Bertram said, as he sat across the table. "What can I do for you, Special Agent Garcia?"

"I need permission from the Mexican Department of Justice to enter their country on official business, but they are adamant that I cannot go to Puebla State."

"You're worried about Lorraine and Ali?"

"Very much so," Garcia said. "I'm not sure that they understand what they're getting into down there."

"I know," Bertram said. "Yesterday Lorraine asked me to call a friend at Foggy Bottom about Arroyo de Riendo and he told me that the place is a sleepy farming village in the shadow of a volcano, and very safe for tourists."

"Right," Garcia said. "There's gruesome drug violence all around but there hasn't been a murder or serious crime committed in that one village in ten years. Does that seem odd to you?"

"Perhaps, but I'm certain that Ransom would not knowingly send his sister and nephew into harm's way."

"How about Connor?"

"Ransom and Connor have a different appreciation of danger," Bertram said. "They seem to enjoy it, which is a personality flaw that I do not approve of."

"Here's the thing," Garcia said. "If Ali's birth mother is in Arroyo de Riendo, some very powerful people will not want her to be found and others would want her killed because she can tell how Ernesto smuggled drugs for Karl Olson, who I'm now sure was a double agent favoring the Russians."

"Then why would she still be alive?" Ransom said. "That's the flaw in your theory, Rene. The Kremlin would have killed Pilar decades ago. And why would Ali be allowed to live? Can you explain that to me?"

"I can't," Garcia said. "Unless the Russians believed that Pilar and Ali were killed in the crash. Ernesto may have arranged for a very secure hideout in Mexico before his final flight, and it may be that the Cubans did not want Pilar and Ali to be harmed. I only know that I need permission to enter Mexico to investigate, and I need it today."

"I doubt that I can be much help with the Mexicans," Bertram said. "The title of ambassador-at-large is mostly an honorarium in recognition of my years at the State Department. They drag me out on occasion to spout off about some international snafu or another on the Sunday morning network television shows, but I no longer have any real authority."

"You could call your son," Garcia said. "I have reason to believe—and this is strictly off the record, sir—that Ransom has strong ties to a very dangerous element in Arroyo de Riendo."

"That is troubling to hear," Bertram said, "but not surprising. I've been worried about Ransom for years, but ever since he came home from Vietnam a changed man, he has chosen to distance himself from me."

"I understand," Garcia said. "This puts me in a tough spot, Ambassador. I'm tempted to go to Arroyo de Riendo without permission from the Mexicans even though the resident FBI agent in Mexico City would not be able to provide backup. The international incident would end my career, which would mean that I'd never be able to prove who put that explosive device on Connor's flight."

"Oh?" Bertram said. "Aren't the Puerto Rican separatists the prime suspect in that bombing?"

"I may be the only one in the FBI who doesn't buy that theory, sir. Lorraine may have told you that we found evidence that Karl Olson was directly involved in a plot to spread chaos in the District of Columbia over thirty years ago."

"Yes," Bertram said. "Speedball Summer."

"I believe that Olson was working for the Russians, Ambassador. He may have been involved in more serious and consequential crimes on their behalf."

"From what Lorraine told me, it sounds like you certainly can connect Olson to the Cubans," Bertram said. "But any connection to Russia is tenuous at best. Unless you have something you're not telling us."

"I do have one thing," Garcia said. "We all know that the Russian Special Forces—the *Spetznaz*—used a disabling gas to end the Chechen terrorist attack on a Moscow theatre three year ago even though the anesthetic effect was so strong that some of the hostages died. Do you recall what chemical agent was used?"

"That was the manufactured narcotic fentanyl," Bertram said.

"Yes, but more precisely an analogue of fentanyl that lends itself to gasification. Naturally, our military was quite concerned that the Russians had chemical agents that might be used against our own troops, so they managed to obtain samples of that chemical for analysis."

"Where are you going with this, Rene?"

"The fentanyl that the *Spetznaz* used in the Moscow theatre hostage rescue had the identical chemical signature of the fentanyl that was mixed with cocaine and distributed on the streets of Washington three decades ago," Garcia said. "The drugs were manufactured in the same lab, and that puts Russian fingerprints all over the chaos of Speedball Summer."

La Cantina

"What about the volcano?"

Lorraine asked this when they were walking across the dusty street to the *cantina* with the slopes of the mountain looming over the town. The red-faced man called Martillo and two of Leona's foot soldiers followed a few paces behind.

"What about it?" Leona said.

"Popocatepetl is active, isn't it? What happens to the town if there is an eruption?" "El Popo isn't much trouble," Leona said. "Now and then he smokes and there is fire at the top, but not too much. The ash came down and killed the crops a few years ago, that's all."

"But what if there is a really big eruption?" Jaime asked.

"Then the slow ones die," Leona said. "And the rest of us run away."

The *cantina* was dark and quiet under a rickety tin roof that extended over a patio. The only other customers were a group of graying hipsters from Minneapolis—leftovers from the '60s—who were staying in the rooms behind the bar.

"Are you guys here for the mushrooms?" a man who was too old to wear his tie-dyed shirt said. "We're finding good ones all over the place."

"No thanks," Bernardo said. "We're just on vacation."

"Are you narcs?"

"No," Lorraine said. "We're just in town for a day or two."

The group sat at a long table near the bar and ordered beers, except for Connor, who had to settle for a Coke. Leona sat at a table against the wall with Martillo and her two men closer to the street. She still carried the big revolver in a shoulder holster and her assault rifle on her lap.

"That guy Martillo gives me the creeps," Ali said.

"He should," Connor said, "if that name means what I think it does."

"El Martillo," Jaime said, "the hammer."

"Great," Nathan said. "Let's get the hell out of here."

"Relax," Lorraine said. "They have our airplane and our money so if they wanted to harm us they would have done it by now."

"Unless they will hold us for ransom," Bernardo said. "Leona may know that Bertram Calhoun is a man of considerable wealth and that my law practice has a high net worth."

"I guess I'll go talk to her," Connor said as he touched Lorraine's hand and stood up.

"Be careful," Lorraine said. "She looks like a stick of dynamite with a short fuse to me."

Connor smiled at Martillo as he walked across the *cantina*. The red-faced man did not return the gesture.

"Mind if I join you?" he said at Leona's table.

"Sit," Leona said. "Ransom said you were like a brother to him."

"Brother-in-law," Connor said. "Ransom and I were in the Navy together. Lorraine is his sister."

"He also said you were boring," Leona said. "I think he called you a flying bus driver, whatever that means."

"I have my moments."

"Oh?" Leona said. "Is this little adventure one of them?"

"Sure," Connor said. "This isn't a bad deal. But you haven't told me how you know Ransom."

"Does it matter? Have another drink," Leona said. "What is that?"

"Just a Coke."

"Coke? You're no good for me," Leona said, dismissing him. "I can't trust a man who doesn't drink." Then Leona pointed at Ali and said, "Send her over here."

"Fine," he said, before walking to where the group was sitting. "We'll talk later.

"Okay, that was a waste of time," Connor said when he was again seated between Lorraine and Ali. "She wants to talk to you, Vasquez."

"Must be my lucky night," Ali said.

Martillo stood up at the same time as Ali and looked toward her, but he walked past to approach two young girls as they entered the *cantina*. At first Ali thought he might be telling the girls they were too young to sit at the bar but instead he put his arms around both of them and went through a curtain into a back room, holding their rear ends.

When Ali turned away, she saw that Leona was not looking at Martillo and the girls.

No, Leona was looking directly at Ali's eyes.

"*Tu, sientate,*" Leona said when Ali stood at her table.

"I don't speak Spanish," Ali said as she took the chair across the table from the other woman.

"No? But you sat down when I told you to."

"It seemed like the thing to do."

"How is it that the one *senorita* in this group that Ransom sent to me doesn't speak Spanish?"

"My family was from Cuba," Ali said. "But I'm an American girl."

"Cuba?" Leona said, shifting the black assault rifle in her lap. "Now I understand, you are more *europeo* than Latin."

"I don't know that much about my family," Ali said. "Although I do suppose they came to Cuba from Spain, but that was a long time ago."

"If you say so," Leona said. "And how about the one you call Bernardo? He looks respectable and rich. How much money does he have?"

"I don't know. He is a very good lawyer in Miami."

"But he's not your fiancé. That was a lie."

"Maybe. We're still working on our relationship."

"Only a *gringo* would say something stupid like that. Working on what? You're screwing his brains out to get that big diamond ring."

"I think we come from different worlds, Leona."

"In my world I could take your Bernardo as my own."

"If we have nothing to talk about," Ali said, "I'll go back to my table."

"Nobody walks away from me," Leona said. "Not even you with your big green eyes."

"Then let's talk about something else."

"Okay. Tell me about your captain, Connor."

"We are both pilots," Ali said. "We work together, that's all."

"He is very direct, very bold. I like that."

"Then why did you send him away?"

"His wife is right there. This wasn't the time."

"There won't be a right time for you and Connor, if that's what you're thinking about."

"Anybody can be had at the right time."

"Can we talk about business, Leona? Don't you want to know why we are here?"

"Later. Now I'm thinking about tonight. How about the boys? Maybe I should take one of them to my room. Or both?"

"That wouldn't work either, Leona."

"Ha! I can see that. So that leaves me with you and your green eyes, Ali."

"I don't think so," Ali said.

"No? You never thought about another woman?"

"Maybe if Bernardo doesn't measure up," Ali said. "But not tonight."

"Of course, Bernardo," Leona said. "Safe, secure Bernardo."

Then Leona stood up and held her assault rifle at her side when she turned to her pair of armed men.

"Come with me, *amigos*," she said. "You have work to do."

The Garrison

Leona had assigned three rooms in her garrison to the group. Each had bunk beds, bars on the windows, and a heavy wooden door that opened to the central courtyard.

"The bathroom is over there," Lorraine said, pointing to an open doorway across the garrison. "It's not the Ritz but it's not as bad as I expected either. There is even a shower."

"Except that there doesn't appear to be a door," Ali said. "What if one of Leona's men comes walking in?"

"Right," Connor said. "One of us will have to stand guard when you gals are in there."

"This place is starting to give me the creeps," Nathan said, looking into one of the assigned rooms. "What if Leona comes by in the middle of the night and locks these doors? We'd be her prisoners."

"We are already her prisoners," Bernardo said. "There are a lot of heavily armed men between us and the airport. Despite what she said about leaving whenever we wish, we won't be getting near that airplane until Leona gives the word."

"To tell the truth," Ali said, "I'm more concerned that there are no deadbolts on the inside of these doors."

"We probably don't have much to fear inside this garrison," Lorraine said. "Leona is protecting us, as far as we know."

"Leona is the one I'm worried about," Ali said. "After our little conversation I'm concerned that she might come creeping into Bernardo's bunk in the middle of the night—or mine."

"That won't be a problem," Bernardo said. "There's only room in the bottom bunk for you and me. Leona is on her own."

"Come on," Jaime said, walking past Nathan into one of the rooms. "Let's put our stuff in here. This will be fun."

"Okay," Nathan said. "I call bottom rack."

"Whatever."

CHAPTER

10

Saturday, March 26, 2005

La Iglesa

Lorraine spent the night close to Connor under a harsh wool blanket on the narrow bunk in their cell. They slept with their clothes on, which did not deter him from quickly slipping into a deep sleep, while she got up several times to peer between the bars on the window and to check that their door had not been locked from the outside.

Well before dawn she walked across the garrison to the latrine without seeing another soul, before she opened the door to the boys' room and awakened them.

"Get up, Nathan. Quietly, please."

"What is it, Mother?"

"Come outside," Lorraine said. "I want you to hear real silence."

"Okay," Nathan said as he stood up and tried to turn on a light. "But the power is out."

"The guards told me they shut off the generator at ten o'clock every night," Lorraine said. "Just put on your shoes and come with me."

"I'm coming, too," Jaime said.

"Sure," Lorraine said. "But let's keep very quiet."

As soon as they were outside Jaime turned on his cell phone and held it up to the stars.

"Put that away," Lorraine said. "We're a hundred miles from the nearest cell tower."

"Just checking," Jaime said.

"Let's see if the gate is locked," Lorraine said.

"I'm pretty sure Leona posted a guard," Nathan said.

"Shush," Lorraine said. "Let's have a look."

They found the guard dozing on a bench outside Leona's office, and Lorraine signaled the boys to pass quietly toward the chain-link gate, which was not locked. Nathan lifted the bar and the three slipped out onto the paving stones of the road.

Arroyo de Riendo was dark and silent, sleeping.

"This place is dead," Jaime said.

"Not for long," Lorraine said. "These farmers will be up before dawn."

"Where are we going?" Nathan said.

"Just next door," Lorraine said. "I want to have a look inside the church."

The church was a small adobe building, much smaller than Leona's garrison, although the bell in the steeple was higher. Lorraine listened at the door and heard nothing before she opened it and shined her flashlight inside, sweeping the beam along empty pews and shuttered windows to the altar, and then back to the confessional booth at the back wall.

"What are you looking for?" Nathan said, looking over his mother's shoulder.

"I'm not sure," Lorraine said. "But I'm certain I heard noises in here a few hours ago."

"It sure looks empty now," Nathan said.

"Maybe you heard a wolf or a coyote sniffing around outside," Jaime said.

"These were human voices," Lorraine said.

They were about to go inside when the guard from the garrison came behind them and grabbed Nathan and Jaime by their scruffs.

"No!" the armed man said. "Stay out!"

"Disculpe, senor," Lorraine said. "Excuse me, we just wanted to see inside."

"No." The guard pushed the boys back toward the garrison. "No!"

When the guard pushed them inside the gate at the garrison and motioned them to their cells, Jaime smiled innocently and said, "*Buenas noches, senor.*"

"*Buenas noches,*" the guard said as he sat back down on his bench.

"That was too intense," Nathan said as they walked in.

"I thought we were going to get shot," Jaime said.

"I think Leona's men have strict orders not to shoot us," Lorraine said. "Although we probably shouldn't push our luck too often. Good night, boys."

The Hunt

The cacophony of roosters crowing in every courtyard in town awakened Connor before the sun.

"Peaches," he said, "where did you wander off to last night?"

"I just wanted to check out the nightlife," she said. "But the guard ushered us back into the garrison."

"Us?" Connor said. "I hope you didn't take Nate on your walkabout. There's no telling how he'd react in a tight corner."

"Nathan was fine," Lorraine said. "Besides, I don't think we have too much to fear from Leona's men, since Ransom wouldn't send us into a truly dangerous situation."

"You're probably right," Connor said. "But we shouldn't hang around here too long. If we get a good look at everything today, let's plan on flying out tomorrow morning."

The muffled notes of the diesel generator starting echoed across the garrison not long after the roosters, bringing Ali and Bernardo out of their room.

"Good morning," Ali said. "Maybe we can get some breakfast at the *cantina* before you two go hunting with Leona."

"How about the boys?" Bernardo said. "Should we wake them up?"

"Let them sleep," Lorraine said. "They'll do their own thing in town today."

The same guard smiled at Lorraine when he opened the gate for the group to walk over to the *cantina*, where they found hot tortillas and eggs. The mushroom hunters were nowhere in sight.

"Are you ready for *la caza*?" Leona said when she joined them. *The hunt.*

"Sure," Connor said. "Let's go."

Leona was leaving the *cantina* with Connor and Bernardo when she turned to Lorraine and Ali and said, "My men will take the rest of you up to the Arroyo before noon."

The hunters climbed into the backseat of Leona's quad-cab truck with a half-dozen men sitting in the cargo bed. Most of the farmers had walked into the fields not long after the roosters called, but some of the stragglers had to jump out of the way when the truck came rumbling up the narrow dirt paths with cornstalks brushing the fenders on both sides.

"We'll stick to the lowlands and hunt birds today," Leona said. "The bigger game will be tomorrow, higher on El Popo."

"What about our guns?" Bernardo said.

"My men have them," Leona said. "They will hand them to you when it is time to shoot, loaded and ready to go."

"That's fine for the shotguns," Connor said. "But we ought to sight in our rifles now, just in case we see a deer or a pig today."

"As you wish," Leona said, ordering her driver to stop the truck. Then two of her men hopped out of the truck and ran up the path a short distance where they laid two cardboard vegetable boxes on the ground.

"Adjust your sights here," Leona said when they dismounted and her men handed Connor his rifle. "It is loaded."

The two men who had set the targets moved a few feet to the side, almost into the corn off the narrow path.

"Not with your men standing there," Connor said.

"You would have to be a terrible shot to miss by two feet," Leona said.

"Right," Connor said. "But it just isn't safe to shoot with people downrange."

"Give me that rifle," Leona said, grabbing the Remington from Connor and pulling it into her shoulder. She quickly fired and worked the bolt-action for a second shot and her men waved casually when both boxes jumped away in puffs of dust on the path near their feet.

"That's good shooting," Bernardo said.

"Your sights are perfect," she said, when she handed the rifle back to Connor.

"Fine," he said.

"Let me give you a bit of advice," Leona said as she climbed back into the front seat. "Don't get in any gunfights while you are down here because you will hesitate like that, and you will die."

"I wouldn't worry about that," Connor said. "I'm spring-loaded to shoot when I have to."

Then before Connor handed the rifle back to the men in the truck, he raised it to his shoulder and looked through the telescopic sights at one lonely stone building higher on the side of the mountain.

Connor was still standing outside the truck when one of the men said, "*Mira!*" and pointed to the top of the mountain towering above them. The men were chattering excitedly and El Popo was smoking once again, exhaling a solid white plume into the blue sky.

"That doesn't look good," Bernardo said.

"El Popo may smoke for days or weeks," Leona said.

"If you're not concerned, I'm not concerned," Connor said as he handed the rifle to the men in the truck and climbed into the backseat with Bernardo. He would have to wait until later to tell the others that there was a small white cross atop the lonely building high on the slopes of Popocatepetl.

Los Monjas Locas

Connor and Bernardo left their guns with Leona's men when then they arrived back at her garrison. Then the two men went across the street to join Lorraine and Ali in the *cantina*.

"Is it safe to be here now that El Popo is smoking?" Lorraine said.

"Leona isn't concerned," Connor said. "Apparently this happens from time to time."

"How was the hunting?" Ali said.

"Dusty and boring," Bernardo said. "How was your trip to the spring?"

"It's more of a dry gulch than a spring," Ali said. "But it was nice to get out and look around, even with armed guards watching our every move."

Connor said, "Where is Nathan?"

"The boys didn't go up to the spring with us," Lorraine said. "They stayed in town all day. I think they are back in Leona's garrison now."

"How about your day?" Bernardo said. "Did you find anything interesting in town?"

"We didn't see any sign of Pilar," Ali said. "Local women avoided us, but I made some discreet enquiries about women with green eyes like mine, with no luck."

"The church was the only place we didn't get a look at," Lorraine said.

"Right," Connor said. "Here comes Leona now. Let's ask her about it."

Their guide came into the *cantina* with her two men and nodded at the group before she sat at her table. When Lorraine approached her, she said, "What do you want now?"

"Leona," Lorraine said, "would it be possible to see inside the church?"

"Do you want to light a candle? You should pray to me. I'm keeping you alive."

"I'm not much on lighting candles," Lorraine said. "But it might be nice to have a quiet moment in there. Your men wouldn't allow that."

"My men were looking out for you," Leona said. "Sometimes travelers stay the night in the church. It isn't good to startle them."

"It looked empty to us."

"Okay, you want a look?" Leona said. "Let's go look."

The group rose from their table and followed Leona across the street to the church, where their guide pushed the heavy door aside and said, "See? There is nothing. You can come anytime when it is light, but not too early."

"Right," Connor said, without crossing the threshold. "It looks like an empty church. Now can we get some chow?"

"Food sounds good to me," Bernardo said.

"Let's get the boys first," Lorraine said, after she had walked around the perimeter of the building, past the shuttered windows and around the pews up to the altar, and back past the confessional.

Leona shrugged and went back to the *cantina* when the group went next door to her garrison, where they found Nathan and Jaime napping with their backs against the adobe wall in the shade outside their cell.

"Rise and shine," Connor said, when he tapped his toe against Nathan's foot to wake him. "How can you guys sleep all day?"

"Not all day," Jaime said. "We have a surprise for you."

"Make it snappy," Connor said. "The rest of us had a busy day. We're starving."

"What are you two so giddy about?" Lorraine said when Jaime went into their cell.

"You'll see," Nathan said.

Jaime was holding a small canvas when he came out of their cell. When he turned the painted side toward them, he said, "The oil is barely dry on this one."

"Oh my God," Ali said. She took the canvas in her hands and held it up. "This is Pilar."

The painting had Mary holding the infant Jesus in front of verdant mountains that were more the Sierra Maestra than the volcanic slopes of Popocatepetl, with a number of stars on either side of the crescent moon.

"Where did you get this?" Lorraine said.

"At the market," Jaime said. "It was on a table, in the open."

"We paid two dollars for it," Nathan said.

"If this is truly a Vasquez original, you made the art purchase of the century," Bernardo said. "It could be worth ten thousand dollars."

"Easily twenty thousand," Jaime said, "if we find a lost artist."

"Slow down," Connor said. "The question is, where did this painting come from, before the market?"

"They said it came from *los monjas locas*," Nathan said.

"The crazy nuns?" Connor said.

"Yes, but they also say that there is no convent in Arroyo de Riendo," Jaime said. "It's hard to explain."

"I think I know," Connor said. "Put that painting out of sight and we'll go to the *cantina*." After the group crossed the street to the little eatery, Connor said, "Just sit down and eat. Let me talk to Leona."

"No way," Ali said. "I want to hear this."

"Me too," Lorraine said.

"We can't all go," Connor said. "It might be a fool's errand to gang up on Leona." He turned to Bernardo. "Nardo, will you stay here with the boys?"

"Of course," Bernardo said. "Although if you piss off our host, even this might not be a safe distance from her machine gun."

"I'll choose my words with that in mind," Connor said when he and the women walked to their guide's table.

"You again?" Leona said when Connor approached her table. "Why do you keep bothering me?"

"We have to go to the convent," Connor said.

"Finally, we know why you are here," Leona said, with a smirk. "First the church, now some convent. Are you religious pilgrims?"

"What we are looking for is in the convent," Connor said.

"There is no convent in Arroyo de Riendo."

"I saw a cross atop one of those white buildings on the mountain," Connor said.

"That's not Arroyo de Riendo. That's another place. We don't go up there."

"Why not?"

"That place is not for us."

"My mother is up there," Ali said. "I'm sure of that. I'm going now."

"You wouldn't get far, *novia*" Leona said. "Even I can't go there."

"Why not?" Lorraine said. "You've got the biggest army in these parts."

"It's an understanding," Leona said. "A convenient truce. I don't bother them and they don't bother me."

"You're afraid of the nuns?" Connor said.

"Not the nuns," Leona said. "Their place is at the entrance to a hidden valley where the others live. Their army is bigger."

"Who are the others?" Lorraine said.

"You know who they are," Leona said, pointing to the faint scar on Lorraine's temple.

"Narco-terrorists?" Lorraine said.

"I suppose you could call them that," Leona said.

Connor said, "Why don't you call the *Federales* to rout them off the mountain?"

"Why would I want to make a crazy move like that?" Leona said. "We have an understanding. There are no murders in Arroyo de Riendo, no executions, no bloody attacks on a child's birthday party. There are seven boulders in a narrow pass below the convent. We call them *las siete hermanas*, the seven sisters, and that is the border between our territories."

"So you do talk to the nuns," Ali said.

"I don't," Leona said, "but the women of the town take things up to them, food and clothing. Whatever the nuns need, the women leave at their door and come back down the mountain. They are the only ones allowed past *las siete hermanas*."

"Do the nuns ever come into the town?"

"No. Sometimes the nuns leave woven blankets or paintings at the door for the women to bring back to town. The paintings are always sold to the mushroom hunters who pass through our town, because nobody in Arroyo de Riendo wants a crazy nun's painting hanging in their house."

"The boys found one of those paintings in the market," Lorraine said. "It was almost certainly painted by Ali's mother."

Leona looked at Ali and said, "Your mother is not in that convent."

"She is," Ali said. "I know that now."

"Maybe once," Leona said. "But no more. Any woman in there is no longer your mother. None of them are who they once were—their minds have left their bodies. Nobody is home in their heads. They are the *monjas locas*."

"Leona, I'm going up there," Ali said. "Whether you want me to or not."

"No, that would not be wise. The nuns would not want you there."

"Then tell the women of the town I have to go up to the convent with them."

"Okay," Leona said as she held her machine gun in one hand and stroked Ali's cheek with the other. "I'll try for you, *bonita*. Maybe tomorrow, maybe the next day or the day after that, I'll take you as close as I can. Then you are on your own."

"I want to go tomorrow, at dawn."

"I'm sure you do," Leona said. "And I want to live to see the sunrise after that, so don't do something foolish that will get us both killed."

Reckless Poet

"Dude, *rad barrels* out there tomorrow."

That was the talk among the big wave surfers at Ruggles in the evening when Bennett and Natalie sat above Cliff Walk with Jeremy Croft, watching the waves break on the rocks below.

"You don't want to go out with us in the morning," Jeremy said. "If the storm keeps pumping big swells like this, dawn patrol is going to be epic."

"This is exactly what I've been waiting for," Bennett said. "I have to go out tomorrow."

"Chill out," Natalie said. "You don't have to do anything."

"The day after might be better for you," Jeremy said. "The ocean will lie down after the storm moves offshore."

"Nope," Bennett said. "I'll be here for dawn patrol."

"Then don't come looking for me," Jeremy said. "You're on your own with the Ruggles crew if you try to drop in on their waves tomorrow."

"You said you'd be my wingman," Bennett said. "Remember?"

"Listen to him, Ben," Natalie said. "The old guys have been waiting for waves like these for years. They're not going to share them with you."

"Nobody owns the ocean," Bennett said.

"Tomorrow won't be an ordinary day at Ruggles," Jeremy said. "All the big names will be out there at first light, pushing to catch their wave."

"When are you going out?" Bennett said.

"A little later," Jeremy said as he stood up to leave their perch. "When it's not so crowded."

"Right," Bennett said. "Like you said, every man for himself."

Bennett and Natalie sat on the rocks in silence for a few minutes after Jeremy left them, until she said, "I have a bad feeling about this, Ben."

"Why?" he said. "That's not what I feel, at all."

"What do you really feel, Ben? You never tell me."

"I feel like my wave out there, over the horizon and far out at sea."

"Come to the sleepover at Tiffany's house, Ben. We can be alone all night in the boathouse."

"There's no heat in her family's boathouse, Nattie. And my wave is building out there. Don't you see? It's rising from a storm two hundred miles away, coming for me."

"We don't need heat, Ben. I'll give you the night of your dreams if you just stay with me in the morning."

"Well, of course—but don't you feel the energy of the ocean?"

"You're thinking with your poet's brain, Ben. One wave is just like any other, but you'll hurt yourself for some crazy notion."

"Maybe I am crazy but I can see my wave now, rushing toward us in the night."

"Why do you do this to me?" Natalie said. "Can't you see I'm afraid for you?"

"I'm afraid I won't be there to ride my wave, Nattie. I'm afraid I'll miss it and it will wash past Ruggles without me and be gone."

"I love you, Ben. But I can't live with a reckless poet."

The Confessional

Nathan and Jaime were still admiring Pilar's painting—and laughing about school and their families the way new friends do—when the diesel generator at the back of the garrison clattered and banged to a stop.

"Ten o'clock?" Jaime said as the single light bulb hanging from a wire in the center of their cell—as well as all the lights in town—faded to darkness.

"On the dot," Nathan said.

"Okay," Jaime said as he rolled to his side. "Good night."

Nathan studied the painting by flashlight for a time before he shook Jaime's shoulder and said, "We need a bible."

"There's a big old bible in the church next door," Jaime said. "We can look at it tomorrow."

"Why wait? We know that the bees' nest painted in the foreground must be a reference to gathering honey in Proverbs and that the stars tally to seventeen and six. So Proverbs chapter 17, verse 6. Doesn't a good Catholic boy like you wonder what that says?"

"If I was a good Catholic boy, I'd know all those verses. But I'm not."

"Good, or Catholic?"

"Both," Jaime said. "I mean, neither."

"Well, I'm going to go next door and look it up."

"That old bible is in Spanish."

"I can read Spanish," Nathan said.

"Like a sixth-grader," Jaime said. "We'll both go, tomorrow."

"You can stay," Nathan said when he crouched by the heavy door to their cell, peering out to the courtyard. "Or you can come with me. The guard just left the gate to go into the bathroom."

"Why do you have to be like that?" Jaime said when he tumbled off the bunk and pulled on his sneakers to follow Nathan out the door. "You're going to get us shot."

"Shush," Nathan said as they walked across the garrison. "Getting back in is going to be the hard part."

"This place is a ghost town," Jaime said when the duo slipped out through the unguarded gate and paused on the empty street, taken aback by the silence. Then they went quickly to the church and stepped inside, where Nathan swept the beam of his flashlight around the pews and shuttered windows until the light landed on the altar.

"Here it is," Nathan said when they stood before the large book.

"*Proverbios*," Jaime said after he unclasped the cover and found their verses. "Start children off the way they should go, and even when they are old they will not turn from it."

"Another verse about children," Nathan said.

"Okay," Jaime said. "Are you satisfied now? Because before we go back to Leona's fortress I want to sit in the priest's chair."

"Whatever floats your boat," Nathan said when he shined the flashlight on Jaime in the high-back chair. "By the way, you look ridiculous."

"How about here?" Jaime said when he stepped to the pulpit. "This thing is huge for such a tiny church."

"Some priest you'd be," Nathan said. "You can't even see over the pulpit."

"That's okay," Jaime said. "There's a little stool under here."

"That's cute," Nathan said. "But it's time to go."

"No way," Jaime said. "Want to have some fun? Let's get in the confessional."

"I don't think so."

"Tell me about your sins," Jaime said, taking the priest's seat behind the curtain.

"I'm not Catholic," Nathan said, stepping into the other side. "And you're not a priest."

"When did you last have sex, my son?"

"What? I'm not going to tell you that."

"Uh, actually, come over here," Jaime said. "I want to show you something."

"Quit kidding around, Jaime. We've got to get back into the garrison."

"No, really. You've got to see this."

Then they were both kneeling outside the confessional examining the floor, which was loose. When they pulled the edge of it up, Nathan shined his flashlight down under the priest's seat.

"What the heck is this?" Nathan said.

"Yahtzee!" Jaime said. "It's a secret passage."

"It's something," Nathan said. "Maybe a place to hide from *los banditos*."

"Give me the flashlight," Jaime said. "I'm going in."

"Holy shit," Jaime said after he dropped into the hole and shined the flashlight beam into the darkness. "You won't believe this."

"What is it?"

"This place is full of—drugs!"

"Jaime, get out of there," Nathan said. "I hear someone outside."

"What?"

"I hear voices outside," Nathan said. "Someone is coming."

"Get down here," Jaime said. "And close that hatch."

"I must be crazy," Nathan said when he dropped into the void and reached over his head to close the floor of the confessional. "They're going to find us here, you know. Then we're dead."

"No, follow me," Jaime said as he clambered on top of the tightly packed bundles that filled the subterranean cavern almost to the ceiling. They crawled under a corrugated steel roof braced with timbers and found a space at the far end where they could drop to the floor.

"I'm going to kill you," Nathan said when he squeezed his lanky frame into the tight space behind the bundles. "If we ever get out of here."

"Quiet," Jaime said as he switched off the flashlight. "Here they come."

They heard the hinges on the floor of the confessional squeak when it was opened from above. Then someone dropped down and began stacking more bundles onto the pile.

Nathan immediately recognized the voice of a woman from above when she said, *"Arriba."* After which the worker climbed out of the hole and the hatch was shut.

"Was that Leona?" Jaime said.

"Hell yes, that was Leona," Nathan said. "Our guide is a *narco*, my friend."

"Let's get out of here."

"No," Nathan said. "Let's wait until dawn."

"What if they come back?"

"I don't think they'll empty this whole room out tonight," Nathan said. "It seems like they're stocking up for a shipment. So, let's wait. We'll stand a better chance of getting back into the garrison—without getting shot—in daylight."

"It could be worse," Jaime said, reaching into his pack. He unwrapped a piece of hard candy for himself and handed another to Nathan. "At least we have some candy down here."

CHAPTER

11

Sunday March 27, 2005

El Ruso

"There is a Russian here," Leona said when she crept into Connor and Lorraine's cell before dawn and laid a hand on Connor's shoulder to awaken him.

He slipped out of bed without disturbing Lorraine and when he was outside with Leona, Connor said, "Do you know where this Russian is?"

"He was seen in a *cabana* nearer to El Popo," she said. "A small, abandoned house on the road up to your convent."

"Is he there now?"

"I am going to investigate."

"Fine," Connor said when he went inside the dark cell to gather his shoes. Lorraine appeared to be sleeping so he kissed her head without a word before he left her.

Leona's truck was parked in front of the hotel, but the customary armed men were not sitting in the cargo bed when she slipped behind the wheel herself. The straps of her shoulder holster nearly pushed her breasts out of the skimpy tank top she wore, and she kept her assault rifle on her lap.

"We're going alone?" Connor said as he avoided stepping on the sawed-off double-barrel shotgun on the floorboard under the passenger seat.

"You'll see," she said.

They were on a narrow dirt lane before another truck pulled out of the darkness and followed them at a distance. The path led toward El Popo over rolling hills with fields of corn on both sides.

"How did you know I was after a Russian?" Connor said.

"I didn't," she said, "until some of my farmers reported that there was a Russian near my town yesterday, asking about you."

"Asking about me?"

"Asking about your whole group," Leona said. "But especially the captain, the American who always takes control."

"In that case, I know this Russian."

"What will you do if we find him?"

"I'm going to kill him."

"Then you'll need this," Leona said when she handed a pistol to Connor.

This was the Glock she had taken from him when they arrived in Arroyo de Riendo, so he deftly checked the ammunition in the magazine and pulled the slide back to verify that it was ready to fire. Then he leaned forward to shove the weapon into the small of his back.

"You handle that pistol like a gunfighter," Leona said.

"I'd rather settle things with my hands," Connor said. "But a man ought to know how to shoot."

"I may have underestimated you," Leona said as she turned off the lights and slowed the truck just before the crest of a hill. "Maybe your Russian isn't going to kill you tonight after all."

"Not if I can help it."

"Let's play hide-and-seek," Leona said when she shut off the motor and panned the area around the *cabana* with a night vision scope. "I don't see any sign of him, unless he is behind the adobe walls. This scope is very sensitive to heat, so he's not hiding in the corn outside to ambush you."

"Good to know," Connor said.

"You understand that you're on your own?" Leona said. "Don't expect any help from me or my men. I'm the chief of police, not a hired assassin."

"Right, this is between me and him," Connor said as he reached for the sawed-off shotgun on the floorboards. "But I'll take all the help I can get. Mind if I borrow this?"

"That's full of buckshot," Leona said.

"Perfect," he said.

"*Buena suerte*, Connor."

He didn't feel the need to say *gracias* as he walked toward the abandoned house with his pistol in the small of his back and Leona's shotgun in his hands. If he was lucky, Volkov would be sleeping and hoping to ambush the group in the morning on their way to the convent, which he had to know was their ultimate destination. If he was unlucky, the Russian would have the advantage of cover and concealment, so this was no time for hesitation.

Sorry, amigos, Connor thought as he closed the last ten paces to the small adobe cottage, which looked as if it had been abandoned long ago. *If you're just farmers in there instead of Volkov, this is just the wrong place, wrong time for you.* Adios.

His movements were sure and quick when he stepped up to a window opening and pointed the shotgun at the darkest shadows under a corner of the roof that had caved in. In an instant both barrels spit flames and a deadly hail of pellets in rapid succession, giving Connor the reassuring back-kick of a powerful weapon discharging properly in his grasp. Then he tossed the empty shotgun down and sidestepped with both hands on his pistol, using the doorjamb as a barricade to look inside. There was no motion in the shadows and no sound other than the ringing in his ears from the two thunderclaps he had let loose.

Leona drove up as Connor was exiting the *cabana* after searching inside.

"Well?" she said. "Was anyone in there?"

"Not a soul," Connor said as he picked up her shotgun and handed it to her.

"But you would have killed your Russian with no warning?"

"Why not? He didn't give me any warning when he tried to kill my family."

"Now I understand," Leona said. "Get in the truck, Connor. I will double the guard on my garrison so that your family is safe inside."

"Fin de la alerta!" Leona said when she picked up her radio to give the all-clear to her men, along with instructions to double the guard.

"Right," Connor said. "I'll keep my pistol handy, too."

"Put it on the dashboard for now," she said as she backed the truck a short distance into the corn and shut off the lights and the engine. "We have something to talk about, Connor."

"What's on your mind?"

"You," Leona said. She placed her assault rifle on the dashboard alongside Connor's pistol and pulled his head toward hers. In a moment she had her hand inside his pants.

"This isn't the right time for this," Connor said.

"Relax, Connor. My men are watching with night vision. No one can approach us without them seeing."

"We should get back to your garrison," he said.

"Not until you have done your duty, Captain."

Then she pulled her tank top over her head and was on top of him, with her shoulder holsters dangling alongside her bare breasts. She yanked forcefully at his belt and zipper and pried his mouth open with her tongue in a wet embrace.

Connor's mind went blank when he reached up and tore her jeans open, sending buttons flying as the denim ripped. His mouth went to her huge nipples and there was grunting and moaning and kicking at the doors of the cab.

The truck rocked for half an hour.

Their furor had naturally subsided into deep breathing when Connor heard a sudden rumble in the distance, like an express freight train. He was on top by then, and when he raised his head, he became aware of a distant orange glow.

"Damn," he said. "We should get out of here."

The top of El Popo was ringed by hot lava creeping out of the caldera, sending hot rocks into the night like skyrockets while the rumbling from deep within the earth echoed into the night.

The Boathouse

Hours passed in the darkness before Natalie was sleeping soundly on the cot in the boathouse. Then slowly, carefully, Bennett untangled himself from her.

If you go, don't come back, she had said. *I have a terrible feeling about this.*

When they were still very close but no longer touching, he rolled slowly onto his side and pulled his legs free of the blanket, his breathing still matching hers.

You don't mean that, had been his retort.

He sat on the edge of the cot and looked for his clothes in the darkness.

Why must you tempt fate so recklessly? You don't have to prove anything to me and if you love me, nobody else matters.

The boathouse was on the harbor side of Newport, at the water's edge. When he stood and pulled on his pants by the window, he could see the cold black water of the harbor rippling and rising around the pilings on the dock, then falling ever so slightly. The pulse of the ocean.

There were big waves offshore.

"I'll be back," he whispered at the door. "Everything will be okay, I promise."

But he knew then she was the most precious thing in his life that could not last—that their misfortune was to have come of age near the ocean where some people could never turn back from the distant watery horizon, and that he was one of those and she was not.

Then he stepped into the cold air of the breathless night, and he remembered the words she had whispered when they had lain motionless between ecstasy and slumber with his cheek against the warm, moist curve of her neck.

You're a beautiful boy, Bennett. But I can't live with a reckless poet.

Fire on the Mountain

When Connor and Leona arrived at the garrison, they found Lorraine, Ali, and Bernardo standing outside the gate where they had an unobstructed view of the first rays of dawn shining on the snowcapped summit of Popocatepetl, with a heavy plume of white smoke and steam rising from the crater.

"This is a hell of a way to wake up," Bernardo said.

"It might smoke for days or weeks," Leona said.

"Or El Popo might blow his top," Lorraine said, "and bury the town in lava and ash."

"*Quien sabe?*" Leona said as she turned and walked into her garrison. *Who knows?*

"You two should leave with the boys," Bernardo said to Connor and Lorraine, with his arm around Ali. "I'll stay here with Ali."

"Where are the boys?" Connor said.

"I thought they were with you?" Lorraine said.

"I doubt they slept through the sound of that first eruption," Connor said. "They must be around here somewhere."

"Yes, I'm sure they went to find a better view of the summit," Lorraine said. And then, "So, is there a Russian here?"

"What?"

"I heard Leona come into our cell and tell you about a Russian," she said. "So, could it be Volkov?"

"Volkov, here?" Ali said. "That changes everything."

"Take a step back," Connor said. "I didn't see the Russian Leona was talking about. I didn't see anybody."

"Then why did she take you out of our cell?" Lorraine said.

"I don't know," Connor said. "Maybe she just wanted to question me alone, or something."

"Or something? What 'or something' would she drag you out of our bed in the middle of the night for?"

"Let's talk about it later, Peaches. Right now, we have to find the boys and decide our next plan of action."

That was when Nathan and Jaime came out of the church and walked up to the group.

"We're right here," Nathan said. "What's going on?"

"Where have you been?" Connor said.

"Dad, I have something to tell you."

"Later, Nate. Can't you see that El Popo is about to blow his top?"

"You boys look like you slept in a cave," Lorraine said. "Go inside and wash up."

"But—"

"Listen to your mother," Connor said. "Things are going to happen fast now, so pay attention."

"Yes, sir," Nathan said as he and Jaime went into the garrison.

"I can't leave here until I go to that convent," Ali said.

"This might not be the best time for that," Lorraine said. "We can come back after El Popo quiets down."

"I can't get this close and walk away," Ali said.

"Lorraine is right about El Popo," Connor said. "And if Volkov really is here, I'm not sure we can count on Leona to have our backs."

"Ransom wouldn't give us a guide we can't trust," Lorraine said.

"Maybe," Connor said. "But last night she was all in favor of allowing me to settle the score with Volkov on my own while she and her deputies stayed out of it. That's a strange way for a sheriff to operate, don't you think?"

"I take Volkov as another sign that Pilar must be here," Ali said. "He would want to know where Pilar is being held."

That was when Connor cocked his head toward the lower fields and said, "Do you hear that?"

"What?"

"That drumming sound in the distance," Connor said. "That's a Huey helicopter."

"It sure is," Lorraine said.

The drumming grew louder as a minor commotion stirred in the garrison. When Leona drove out with two trucks full of deputies, she stopped by the group and said, "The scientists are coming for El Popo. If you are staying, we will have to modify your sleeping arrangements to make room for them."

"We're still weighing our options," Connor said. "But I'll take a ride to the airport with you to check on our airplane, if you don't mind."

"Get in back," Leona said, and Connor jumped into the truck bed with four heavily armed deputies who shifted their weapons and eyed the *gringo* with suspicion.

The Scientists

Connor went straight to Old Snort when they arrived at the airstrip, so he was standing a short distance away when the helicopter made a circling approach and landed amid a cloud of dust. The markings said *Marina*—Navy—but two civilians stepped out carrying heavy black nylon cases.

Connor walked over to Leona and stood behind the scientists while they loaded their equipment in the bed of her truck. When they all climbed in, they were shoulder to shoulder with Leona's *pistoleros,* and Connor was sitting across from Special Agent Rene Garcia.

"Hi," Connor said, counting on his best poker face to mask his surprise.

"I'm Rene from the University of Texas," Garcia said as he reached to shake hands with Connor as if they had never met. "And this is Doctor Nichelle Cotton from the University of Maryland."

"Interesting job you have," Connor said while the helicopter kicked up another cloud of dust and then took off over their heads. "Coming to a dangerous place when everyone else is running away."

"Volcanos are my life," Garcia said with a wry smile. "Is that your airplane?"

"Yes."

"That thing looks old and worn out," Garcia said. "Are you going to be able to fly it out of here when the lava starts to flow?"

"Old Snort is a damn good airplane," Connor said. "How else would she get to be so old?"

"In that case you should probably take off as soon as you can. As a volcanologist I'd have to say that we may see a major eruption at any time. Wouldn't you agree, Doctor Cotton?"

"Absolutely," Nichelle said. "We should also depart to a safer location as soon as we complete our measurements."

"I'll have to talk to the other members of my party about that," Connor said. "One of them is reluctant to leave here right away."

"Give us a few minutes to secure our gear," Garcia said. "I'd like to meet them before we go up the mountain."

Connor jumped out of the truck when it arrived at the gate to Leona's garrison and walked across the square to the *cantina*, where Lorraine was sitting with Ali and Bernardo.

"Where are the boys?"

"They're still in the garrison," Ali said. "Wasn't that—?"

"Right," Connor said. "Rene Garcia is in town, and I'm pretty sure that woman is also an undercover agent. They're posing as volcanologists and we're not supposed to know them."

"That's Nichelle Cotton," Lorraine said. "I met her when I was in Baltimore with Garcia."

"Then you'll need to use your acting skills to pretend you've never met," Connor said. "That will be the drill for all of us when Leona or her men are within earshot."

"If those scientists are really FBI agents," Bernardo said, "are they here to help us or arrest us?"

"Garcia has to know that Leona is a crooked cop," Lorraine said. "He must be here to help us. I just wonder what he knows that we don't know."

"We couldn't talk freely in the truck around Leona's men," Connor said. "But Garcia was giving me hints that they want to get us away from here as soon as possible."

"Oh no," Ali said, looking across the square to Leona's fortress. "Nathan and Jaime are coming out of the garrison and they're going to walk right past Garcia."

"Has Nathan ever met this FBI agent?" Bernardo said.

"Yes," Lorraine said. "Garcia interviewed Nathan after the bombing incident on Connor's flight."

The group could only watch as Nathan and Jaime walked toward the FBI agents, who were talking to Leona near her truck. They were only a few paces away when Jaime stopped for a moment so that Nathan could put something in his knapsack, but Garcia turned slightly so that his back was to them and the boys passed without recognizing him.

"That was too close," Ali said, when the boys crossed the square to join them in the *cantina*.

"What was too close?" Jaime said as they sat at the big table under the tin roof.

"Don't look toward the garrison," Lorraine said. "Nathan, do you remember Rene Garcia from the FBI? That was him and another agent you just walked past."

"Really? What is he doing here?"

"We're not sure yet," Connor said. "The main thing is that we can't blow their cover, so we're going to play a little charade where they're scientists here for the volcano and we've never met before. Got it?"

"Sure," Nathan said. "No problem."

"So, what do we do next?" Jaime said.

"I don't know about you," Connor said, "but I'm going to have breakfast. Let's rustle up some ham and eggs."

The group was devouring platters of food when Garcia and Nichelle left Leona and came across the square to the *cantina*.

"Pull up a couple of chairs, professors," Connor said, "and join us for breakfast."

"Right," Garcia said. "But we have to talk quickly, because Leona is right behind us. When she gets here, Nichelle and I are scientists and you've never met us before. Does everyone understand that?"

Nichelle squeezed in between Nathan and Jaime and said, "What's for breakfast, boys?"

"It's all good," Jaime said. "Do you carry a gun?"

"All the time. It's part of the job."

"Well, I don't see where," Jaime said. "I mean, those jeans are pretty tight."

"If I show you my gun, I have to shoot you," Nichelle said. "And we don't want Leona to see that, right?"

"Don't worry about us," Nathan said. "We're good at charades."

"I'll bet you are," Nichelle said. "When Leona gets here, it's showtime, okay?"

"Listen," Connor said, "we're all wondering why you're here."

"We came to get you out of here," Garcia said.

"Leona will let us leave whenever we want," Ali said.

"Not if you see too much," Garcia said. "You must know by now that Leona is up to no good. The Mexican government turns a blind eye to her activities as long as there is no violence in the area. They have bigger fish to fry."

"We haven't seen anything but a peaceful little farming village," Lorraine said. "Although Leona does seem to have a small army on her payroll."

"That's right," Garcia said. "So I advise you to scram before you see too much."

"Uh," Nathan said, "it's sort of too late for that."

"You'd better explain that," Connor said. "Tell it straight up and fast, Nate."

"Well, last night Jaime and I went to the church to look up a bible verse for the new painting, and we found a secret passage full of drugs."

"We'll talk about what you were doing in the church later," Connor said. "What makes you think there were drugs in some secret passage?"

"It's a chamber under the confessional," Jaime said. "And it's full of cocaine."

"That's right," Nathan said. "We had to hide in there ourselves when Leona came to stash more dope. We slept on top of tons of coke last night. It was pretty intense."

"Are you sure it was Leona?" Garcia said.

"Positive," Jaime said. "We heard her voice, and someone called her by name."

"That's what I was trying to tell you," Nathan said. "Leona is a *narco*."

"Great," Lorraine said, dropping her forehead into her hands.

"All right," Connor said. "As long as Leona doesn't know what you saw, we should all get aboard Old Snort and fly away."

"No," Ali said. "I'm not leaving."

"We have to go," Lorraine said. "It doesn't make any sense to stay between a volcano and a drug ring."

"Not while I'm this close to finding Pilar," Ali said.

"In that case I will also stay," Bernardo said.

"You don't have to," Ali said.

"Yes, I do," Bernardo said, holding her hand.

"Ali, you don't understand the enormity of this," Garcia said. "Your search for Pilar has stumbled into something that some very powerful people want to cover up. Leona's narcotics racket is just a sideshow."

"Pilar is in that convent, or whatever it is," Ali said. "I'm sure of that now and I won't leave here until I find her."

"And then what?" Connor said.

"Then I'll—I'll bring her home," Ali said.

"Ali, if Pilar is still alive she would be sixty-six years old," Lorraine said. "She might be in no condition to come down the mountain."

"Then I'll stay with her," Ali said.

"Watch your words," Bernardo said, when one of the mushroom-hunting old hippies approached the group's table. "We have company now."

"Hey, how's everybody today?" the psychedelic enthusiast said. "It looks like a fine day for hunting 'shrooms."

"No thanks," Connor said.

"Aw, come on," the hippie said. "We've seen you out in the fields. Are you going to bring in some big commercial operation and harvest all the mushrooms?"

"Listen, buddy," Connor said. "We don't give a damn about any magic mushrooms. They're all yours, so have a ball."

"That's right, we found this place first," the hippie said, as if he really had the last word. "We've been coming here for years, so you better just forget about taking any of our stuff."

The man in the tie-dyed shirt was still talking—and interrupting the group's last chance to talk freely—when Leona came across the square with Martillo and circled the big table with a squad of her gunmen.

Las Siete Hermanas

"Is there a problem, Clive?"

Leona said this after her gunmen sat down at nearby tables all around the group.

"These guys are trying to move in on our deal," the hipster said.

"You must be tripping," Leona said. "These are hunters and tourists, and the newcomers are scientists here to study El Popo. Go gather all the stinky fungus you want and they won't bother you."

"They better not," Clive said as he went behind the curtain of his room behind the bar.

"Now," Leona said, "it is time to go up to El Popo with your instruments."

"Fine," Garcia said. "According to the topographic map, there is a cluster of small buildings on the middle slopes that might be a good location for our monitors. Can you take us there?"

"The convent?" Leona said, looking at Ali. "What a coincidence. We might as well kill two birds with one stone, as they say."

"Yes," Ali said. "I'm ready now."

"Good," Leona said. "Get in the truck and we'll leave right away."

"Wait," Bernardo said. "I'm coming too."

"As you wish," Leona said. "In fact, why don't all of you join this expedition?"

"Not the boys," Lorraine said. "They should stay here."

"Especially the boys," Leona said. "It is easier for me to keep an eye on them if you all stay together."

"You're sure we'll be safe?" Lorraine said.

"I gave your brother my word that I wouldn't harm you," Leona said. "But you shouldn't go too far up El Popo. Ali alone should go all the way to the convent."

"That works for us," Garcia said. "Our instruments and sensors will work fine if we set up on that flat spot just below the convent."

"Then bring something to drink," Leona said. "It will be a long day on El Popo."

Lorraine and Ali collected some sodas and canned juice from behind the bar and passed them out to the group. Then they all went to the town square where a stake-body truck and two pickups were waiting.

"You will all ride in the big truck," Leona said. "Except Ali, she will be with me."

"Are you sure this is a good idea?" Connor said to Garcia in a whisper as they climbed onto the flatbed of the truck. "They could be taking us anywhere."

"What else can we do?" Garcia said. "But be ready."

"Right," Connor said.

The road to El Popo was fairly straight and passable to the edge of the farmland, but after that it switchbacked up the mountain and became a torturous route, and Connor sensed that their situation was moving from bad to worse. Leona's *pistoleros* were getting edgy as the truck advanced up the slope of the smoking mountain looming over them, and the tension mounted each time the truck bucked and tilted awkwardly as if to violently eject them all. So he silently reassured each member of the group with prolonged eye contact and a calm countenance.

Then the truck jolted to a stop after an especially hard lurch.

"You will have to walk from here," Leona said when she stepped down from the cab of the truck. "You can all go up the path until it narrows between *las siete hermanas*. Only Ali should go past there to the convent."

"Can't we wait here with the truck?" Nathan said.

"No," Garcia said, dismounting from the truck bed and shouldering his case of scientific instruments. "We should all stay together."

"I don't want to go up there," Nathan said.

"Let's stay together," Nichelle said, toting her own equipment case.

"That's right," Garcia said, looking straight at Connor. "You should all come with me."

"I agree," Connor said, sensing that Garcia had a plan. "Let's all stay together."

"Okay," Nathan said, and they all turned toward the path and began walking, with Jaime bringing up the rear—until he jolted to a sudden stop.

"Halt," Martillo said, pulling hard on Jaime's shoulder. "You have something of mine."

"What?"

The group stopped and turned around to see Martillo holding Jaime with his sawed-off shotgun pointed at the boy's head.

"Martillo," Leona said, "leave the little one alone."

"I should shoot this pest now," Martillo said. "He's a thief."

"Take it easy," Bernardo said, reaching toward Jaime. "Nobody needs to get hurt here."

"You think so?" Martillo said. "What about this?"

Then the red-faced *pistelero* spun Jaime around by the arm and reached under the flap of his backpack. When his dirty hand came out, it was holding a plastic-wrapped slab of white powder about the size of a textbook.

"Did you think you could just help yourself?" Martillo said. "I work for this."

"What is it?" Bernardo said.

"Cocaine, you idiot," Martillo said. "When I looked into our storeroom this morning, I saw that one of the bales had been cut open. One little pillow was missing, but the thief left a candy wrapper behind. Didn't you, Jaime?"

"It's not yours," Leona said. "Remember, we all share."

"Not anymore," Martillo said as he snatched the AR-15 out of Leona's hands. The move stunned her, and she began to reach for the big revolver in her shoulder holster before she saw that she was staring down both barrels of Martillo's shotgun, point blank.

"What is this?" Leona said.

"You got your cocaine back," Lorraine said. "Just let us all go, please."

"Come here," Ali said, motioning to Jaime while Martillo was confronting Leona. The boy stepped away from the *pistolero* and stood between Bernardo and Ali, who put their arms around him.

"*Sí*, you should all go up there," Martillo said, nudging Leona with his shotgun. "And you too, Leona. Go with your *gringo* friends."

"Why, Martillo?" Leona said. "Why do you do this?"

"You let these *gringos* come in and take over our town and steal from us," Martillo said. "Besides, your face is drying out and your tits are starting to sag. We don't want you around here anymore."

"You won't get away with this," Leona said.

"It's already done," Martillo said, waving her away with his shotgun. "Go with your *gringos*."

"Let's go," Connor said, motioning the group up the path toward the convent. "There's nothing we can do here."

"This isn't over," Leona said to Martillo before she turned and followed the group on the path.

"Dad," Nathan said, "this sucks."

"You asked to come with us," Connor said. "Now deal with it."

"I'm sorry about the cocaine," Jaime said. "I couldn't stop myself. That little slab of white powder could have paid off my student loans."

"We'll talk about that later," Connor said. "Right now, it's time for you boys to learn some tactics. Rule one is always cover your flanks. So, Nate, you keep an eye to the left, and Jaime, you cover our right side. Watch for movement, sun glare, birds flying, anything. When we stop walking, keep watching your side and maintain the perimeter."

"Dad, you make it sound like we're in a war or something."

"Like it or not, we are in a tactical situation," Connor said. "I need you to get your head in the game, Nate."

"Yes, sir."

They were about two hundred yards from the seven boulders when they heard gunfire behind them. Connor and Garcia said, "Get down!" at the same time, and when the group turned to look back down the path, they saw that the truck was driving down off the mountain with Martillo's men wildly firing their weapons in the air.

"What—?" Nathan said.

"They're calling the animals," Lorraine said. "It's feeding time at the zoo."

"You mean they're serving us to the *narcos*?" Jaime said. "That wasn't nice."

"Enough of that," Connor said. "Let's get organized."

"Connor is exactly right, let's maintain a perimeter and take stock of our situation," Garcia said when the group gathered around. "And, Leona, you can give me your weapon now."

"No," Leona said. But Nichelle was already behind her, holding her by the wrists, while Garcia pulled the big revolver from her shoulder holster.

"You can't do this," Leona said. "You have no authority here."

"Just relax," Nichelle said. "I'll let you go if you behave."

"I knew you were not scientists," Leona said after Nichelle released her. "What are you, DEA? FBI? Or are you mercenaries hired by Ransom Calhoun to get his sister?"

"We're FBI."

"Am I under arrest?"

"No," Garcia said. "I don't have arrest authority here. But you're going to have to come with us unless you know another way off this mountain."

"I'm not leaving El Popo with you," Leona said. "I'm going back to my town to deal with Martillo."

"Listen to me," Bernardo said. "I am a very good lawyer, Leona. You should come with us. I can guarantee you the best representation back in the states or here in Mexico."

"He's right," Ali said. "Coming with us is your best bet, Leona."

"Don't waste your time with her," Connor said. "You can go or you can stay, Leona. Just know that I'm getting my family off this mountain, and if you get in my way, I'll drop you on the spot."

"Dad!" Nathan said. "Stop that."

"Be quiet, Nathan," Lorraine said. "Your father knows what he's doing."

"I agree with Connor," Garcia said. "You're not my prisoner, Leona, but if you interfere with our escape, we'll do what we have to do. Is that understood?"

"I don't have much choice," Leona said. "But I much preferred your manner in my truck last night, Connor."

"Forget that," Connor said, with a glance at Lorraine before he looked to Garcia. "What is our escape route, Rene?"

"Nichelle," Garcia said, "let's have a look at that map."

When Nichelle produced a topographic map from her pack, she spread it on the ground and the group gathered around.

"We're here," Garcia said, drawing a finger across the map to a place where the contour lines spread apart to indicate a flat spot. "And we need to get here, to this little plateau below the convent."

"What happens at the plateau?" Ali said.

"That's how we're getting out of here," Connor said. "A squared-away operator always has an escape route. Isn't that right, Rene?"

"Correct," Garcia said. "We planned several extrication points all around Arroyo de Riendo with the helicopter crew. That plateau was one of them. We call it *santo jardin*."

"I suppose one of us has to ask why?" Nathan said.

"It means 'holy garden,'" Nichelle said. "We think the nuns use that spot as a vegetable garden. There is a very short path—only about twenty-five yards—that leads from there right to the front door of the convent."

"That's perfect," Ali said. "When you call the helicopter back, we can bring Pilar down the path and fly her out with us."

"Ali, please slow down," Bernardo said. "Our main objective today is to escape. There may not be time to negotiate for the release of Pilar."

"What's to negotiate?" Ali said. "She's coming with me."

"There won't be time for that," Connor said. "We're going to have to scramble aboard that helicopter the moment it touches down and scram off this mountain."

"Ali, think about it," Lorraine said. "Pilar might have been in that convent ever since Ernesto's airplane crashed in the Everglades. That's thirty-three years inside those walls, on top of two decades in the *Presidio Modelo* in Cuba. She's been cloistered most of her life and she won't immediately recognize you as her daughter. She may not want to come out with you."

"Pilar will know who I am," Ali said. "And she will come home with me."

"We can deal with that later," Garcia said. "First we have to get to the plateau and call in the helicopter."

"And it's safe to assume that the *narcos* heard all that gunfire from Martillo's crew," Nichelle said. "So they know that someone is on their mountain."

"Which they won't like one bit," Connor said. Then he turned to Leona and said, "Do the *narcos* post lookouts on the far side of those boulders?"

"How the hell would I know?" Leona said. "In all my life I've never been past *las siete hermanas*."

"The women who bring supplies to the convent must know," Lorraine said.

"I'm sure they do," Leona said. "Why don't we go back down to my town and ask them? You could give me back my pistol so I could deal with Martillo, too."

"That's not going to happen," Connor said. "And don't forget, Nikoli

Volkov is somewhere around here. He might even be the spark behind Martillo's mutiny."

"That's certainly possible," Garcia said. "Martillo would have been an easy mark for Volkov. He could have bribed Leona's right-hand man to get rid of us and earn a promotion to king of the hill at the same time."

"If you ask me," Lorraine said, "Volkov will try to ambush us at the seven boulders."

"Right," Connor said, drawing his pistol from the small of his back where it had been concealed under the tail of his shirt. "I'll have to outflank him."

"It won't be easy," Garcia said. "There's not much brush for cover, and there's a lot of loose rock on the slope. If Volkov has a long gun, you'll be a sitting duck out there."

"Somebody has to do it," Connor said.

"Then let's both go," Garcia said. "Do you want left or right?"

"I'll take left," Connor said.

"Good," Garcia said. "Nichelle, you're in charge here. Get on the radio and tell the helicopter pilots we'll be at the holy garden landing zone in thirty minutes. Wait for the all-clear before you come up to the boulders."

"Understood," Nichelle said. "Good luck."

Then Garcia said, "Bernardo, can you handle a revolver?"

"Yes. My father always carried a firearm and I was taught respect and proper handling at a very young age."

"Okay," Garcia said. "Here, take Leona's weapon."

"You can't leave me on El Popo without my pistol," Leona said.

"Just be quiet," Bernardo said. "It was your idea we should all come up here, remember?"

"Connor," Lorraine said, "be careful."

"I'll see you at the boulders," Connor said as he took off sprinting, cutting off the path on a tangent. Then he turned upslope and crouched behind some bushes, where he raised a hand to signal Garcia *all clear*. Then Garcia took off to the right side, and the two men leapfrogged up the slope until they were even with the seven boulders.

"I can't watch this," Ali said, turning away and sitting on the side of the trail. "I never wanted anyone to get hurt for me."

"Ali, there is something you must know," Lorraine said when they sat together. "I've spoken with the man who held Pilar and Ernesto captive in the Sierra Maestra. Commandante Tejera was present on the day you were born."

"What? There is a man who actually knew Pilar and Ernesto when they were in the Sierra, and you didn't tell me?"

"He is very old," Lorraine said, "and Vicente always wished to respect his privacy. We can talk about that later, but what you must know now is this—Ernesto Fuentes could not be your father."

"How can you say such a cruel thing? Ernesto loved Pilar so much he came back to Cuba to gain her freedom. He has to be my father."

"I'm sorry, Ali—I really am—but when you were born, Pilar and Ernesto had only been together for seven months. Tejera is quite certain of that. What's more, he gave his journal to Vicente to prove that you are Pilar's daughter, born in Cuba. Bernardo will find the journal in Vicente's papers eventually, I'm sure."

"No, I don't believe any of that," Ali said.

"Ali, listen to me. Pilar had been severely beaten in Havana before Tejera brought her to the Sierra. It was a miracle that she didn't lose you before you were born—that's how injured she was—but he is certain that you were born only seven months later."

"That's not true," Ali said.

"Ali, you don't want to know this, but you must. It isn't a pretty thought, but Pilar was certainly beaten in Havana before she was brought to Ernesto in the Sierra Maestra. These were very bad men, so anything could have happened. It is dreadful, but who can say that Pilar was not raped in captivity?"

"How can you be so cruel?" Ali said. "That's not true, and I never want to hear that again."

El Santo Jardin

After Connor and Garcia closed on the seven boulders from both flanks and found the pass clear, they signaled the group to come up the path and join them.

"This isn't the spot," Connor said. "But I still think that Volkov is somewhere on this mountain."

"Either way, we're entering the *narcos'* territory now," Garcia said. "Isn't that right, Leona?"

"*Las Siete Hermanas* is the border crossing," Leona said. "There will be trouble if you go any farther."

"The *narcos* let the women from Arroyo de Riendo bring supplies to the nuns," Lorraine said. "Maybe the convent is their actual red line."

"They are watching us now," Leona said. "Any step you take past these boulders may be your last on earth."

"That may be true," Connor said. "The path is steep and there is no cover to speak of. But we don't have any choice."

"Next time you could try picking a better place for the helicopter to land," Nathan said. "I'm just saying, that's all."

"Shut up, Nate," Connor said. "Garcia and Nichelle are risking their lives to get us out of here."

"We had to pick some flat places for the helicopter," Nichelle said. "The pilots were adamant about not picking us off a slope. The *narcos* shoot at any helicopter that gets too close, so they don't want to be hovering around looking for a landing spot."

"Sorry, Nathan," Garcia said. "You can file a complaint with the Bureau later. Right now, we should stay spread out and get up to the landing zone quickly. I'll take point. Are we all ready?"

"I'm right behind you," Connor said. "Let's go."

Garcia led the way followed by Connor, Nichelle, and Leona with Ali, Bernardo, Lorraine, and the boys bringing up the rear. They moved quickly even though the path was steep and strewn with loose rocks, and they all knew they were easy targets for the men with rifles who were certainly watching them.

When they reached the edge of the plateau, Garcia dropped to the ground and motioned for the others to do the same, all of them closing ranks and taking cover behind the slight berm that marked the limit of the garden. The austere walls of the convent were directly above them at the top of a stairway that had been cut into the side of the mountain. There were no signs of life.

"What now?" Ali said.

"Now we wait for the helicopter," Connor said, but a moment later some dirt on the berm jumped and scattered as a bullet struck nearby, and they heard the report of a distant gunshot echo down the slope of Popocatepetl.

"Holy shit," Nathan said. "They're shooting at us."

"Easy now," Connor said. "It was no accident that they missed us by twenty feet."

They were all sweaty from the climb and the noon sun, but Connor also recognized the smell of panic in the group, and he did his best to allay their fears.

"That was just a warning shot," he said, "so everybody stays low."

"Nichelle, did you see the shooter's location?" Garcia said.

"No," she said. "But he must be at least one hundred yards away since the sound of the shot came after the bullet struck."

"They're telling you to go no farther," Leona said.

"Maybe they will allow us to leave," Bernardo said. "It makes no sense for them to invite a full-scale invasion of El Popo if they shoot down the helicopter."

"These *narcos* are *perros locos*," Leona said. *Mad dogs.* "Nothing they do makes any sense."

"Hey," Jaime said. "Do you hear that?"

"Hear what?" Nathan said.

"Listen, I think I hear drumming in the distance, or something."

"That's a Huey helicopter," Connor said. "And it's coming right at us."

"Exactly on schedule," Garcia said. "Be ready to jump onboard as soon as they touch down."

"You can give me my pistol now," Leona said. "I will be staying here."

"Are you sure?" Lorraine said. "Your situation here looks hopeless."

"I will find a way," Leona said. "But I need my pistol."

Bernardo looked to Garcia, who nodded before he handed the revolver back to her.

The sound of the helicopter was drawing closer when Ali suddenly clambered over the berm into the garden.

"No," she said, "I've got to get Pilar."

"Ali!" Lorraine said, making a futile reach for her. "Stay down!"

"Damn it!" Connor said, when he took off after her amid several shots from high on the mountain that landed in the vegetables near his feet. But Ali had enough of a head start to sprint up the steps to the door of the convent before he could grab her.

She was inside the walls before he reached the door.

Connor held his pistol low at his side when he went in. The door opened to a narrow hall with a low arched roof. Ali had not gone far. Nikoli Volkov was holding her from behind, pressing Ali against the stone wall with his hand over her mouth and his pistol pointed directly at Connor's head.

Connor ducked and bobbed instinctively, and the bullet went past his head. In the same motion he pushed the pistol aside with his left hand and cold-cocked the Russian with the butt of his Glock. Volkov staggered and dropped his pistol while Ali gasped, slumped against the wall—he had been smothering her with one hand, but she was breathing again—and then the two men were grappling for survival in the narrow space.

Volkov had Connor's back to the wall with one hand on his neck and the other around his Glock, trying to pry the weapon out of Connor's right hand. Connor knew his situation was desperate, but he didn't even think about his next move.

Some things you never forget.

He raised his fist and his elbow and put his shoulder, hips, and feet into a tight roundhouse punch at Volkov's jaw, the way he had learned to deal with an opponent who had him on the ropes decades earlier. Then another, and another left, and another in rapid succession, using the wall behind his right shoulder for leverage. The Russian let go of Connor's neck and tried to block his punches with his right hand, but Connor had seized the momentum of the struggle and he kept firing roundhouses until Volkov's eyes rolled back and he staggered to his knees.

Connor dragged the Russian out the door of the convent into the sunshine and threw him to the ground. He was on his back and rose to his elbows when Connor raised his pistol and stood above him to administer the *coup de gras*.

"If I had known you were a boxer," Volkov said, "I might have given you some respect."

"Now it's me or you," Connor said as he looked over the sights aimed at Volkov's head, gently squeezing the slack out of the trigger. The helicopter was close by then, making a thumping final approach to the plateau where the others were waiting.

"You can't kill me," Volkov said with a sly smile. "Americans don't shoot an unarmed man."

Damn it, Connor thought. *Why did he have to be right about that?*

The sound of Leona's big revolver firing startled Connor—he hadn't seen her rush up from the garden—but it killed Volkov instantly. Then she was standing over the Russian's corpse, putting the revolver away in her shoulder holster, and looking into Connor's eyes.

"You didn't have to do that," Connor said.

"Go home, Connor," she said.

"You should come with us."

"You better go inside and get Ali," Leona said as the helicopter was touching down in the garden.

Connor bolted into the convent when he saw that Ali had pulled herself together and gone all the way inside. He startled a few nuns who were holding their beads and praying fervently in the chapel, but one of them pointed to a courtyard where Ali was standing next to an old woman who was sitting in front of an easel, patiently picking paint off a palette and putting it on canvas.

"You shouldn't be here," the mother superior said to Connor.

He said, "Is that—?"

"Yes, she is the artist Pilar Vasquez."

"Why are you holding her here?"

"It is Sister Pilar's sincere desire to remain within these walls."

"How did she get here?"

"The sisters from Puebla de Los Angeles brought her to us in search of a secret sanctuary. They feared that some men would kill her if she was found. Are you such a man?"

"No," Connor said. He tucked his pistol into the small of his back and approached Ali and Pilar.

"I am Alicia," Ali said to Pilar. "I am your daughter."

When Pilar looked up, Connor saw that her eyes were as green as Ali's but full of sorrow.

"No," Pilar said. "God took my dearest Alicia to heaven long ago. I will join her there soon."

Connor heard the helicopter on the ground outside the convent and said, "Ali, we have to go now."

"I am here for you now," Ali said, dropping to one knee at Pilar's side. "Mother, look at my eyes. I am Alicia, your daughter."

"No, my daughter was killed in the plane crash with Ernesto."

"Yes," Ali said. "Yes, you must remember. I know that you loved Ernesto dearly and that he was my father. But I was not killed. I am here for you now."

"You are wrong," Pilar said. "Ernesto was not the father of my child."

"But you loved him and he loved you."

"Ernesto and I were always in love. But he was not the father of Alicia."

"Sister Pilar has taken a vow of silence," the mother superior said. "You should leave her now."

"But I must know!" Ali said. "Mother, please tell me, if not Ernesto, who was my father?"

Pilar turned her sad green eyes back to her canvas, raised her brush, and spoke one last word before returning to honor her vow of silence.

"Fidel."

Fate's Surprise

"You're just in time," surfer Jeremy Croft said when Natalie arrived at Ruggles. "Ben is getting set to drop in on a giant wave—a real monster."

"You've got to stop him," Natalie said. "I've got to talk to him."

"Too late. Look, he's going to catch the biggest wave of the day."

"But I just talked to his grandfather and his family is all okay. They're safe now and coming home from Mexico."

She saw Bennett just offshore, paddling furiously and then pushing down the front of a swell that grew into a tremendous wave—the crest well above his head—sweeping in from the sea toward the rocks and shoals behind the Vanderbilt Mansion.

"Nobody in the world can stop him now," Jeremy said as Bennett dropped into the curl of the wave. "He's on his own to ride that monster over the reef—or else."

"Oh boy!" somebody in the crowd of spectators behind them said. "This isn't good!"

"That kid is too small," another said. "He shouldn't even be out there."

"That kid is going to wipe out on the rocks!" another spectator said with a nervous laugh. "He sure better do something quick."

"Too late."

Natalie couldn't exhale when she saw the wave curling full circle over Bennett's head, then crashing down ahead of him. He and his board disappeared in the foamy water near the Cliff Walk as if flushed down into the depths.

"I didn't want him to do this," Natalie said. "I tried everything to stop him."

The board came up between the rocks a few seconds later with no sign of the rider.

"Oh no!" Natalie said. "Somebody help him!"

"I'm going," Jeremy said, grabbing his surfboard. "It might not be too late. He might still come up okay—maybe."

"Oh my God!" Natalie yelled, looking to the churning foam and rocks where he had vanished. "Bennett! Don't let it end like this!"

Then Jeremy was paddling his surfboard in the backwash of the wave and he reached into the water to grasp Bennett's limp form when it rolled to the surface. Even before he reached the shore with the younger surfer's unconscious body laid across his board, sirens and flashing lights announced the arrival of the Newport fire department on Ruggles Avenue.

"Bennett!" Natalie said as the firemen pushed her aside to tend to the injured youth. "It's okay, Ben," she said, "they're all safe in Mexico. They found Ali's mother and they're coming home. Everything is okay."

Bennett rolled his eyes and coughed up some water while the firemen and paramedics cut his wetsuit away and bandaged his knees where the jagged rocks had cut him, while he said, "I can't move my right arm."

The police moved spectators back so that a Coast Guard helicopter could land on the lawn behind the Vanderbilt Mansion, and the rescuers strapped him into a special litter.

"Where are you taking him?" Natalie said.

"The trauma center at Rhode Island Hospital," a helicopter crewman said.

"I love you, Ben," Natalie said. "I'll call Bertram and we'll be there right away."

"You know what this means," Jeremy said, "don't you? You won't be running anymore this season—so my record for the mile run will stand."

"I guess you win, Jeremy," Bennett said, laughing through the pain as they put him aboard, before the gleaming white helicopter roared into the sky. "Damn, the bad luck."

www.dscooperbooks.com

Made in the USA
Columbia, SC
02 May 2023

16020610R00114